TAKEN BY HIM

MEASHA STONE

Copyright © 2020 by Measha Stone

Published by Stormy Night Publications and Design, LLC.
www.StormyNightPublications.com

Cover design by Korey Mae Johnson
www.koreymaejohnson.com

Images by DepositPhotos/SWEviL, DepositPhotos/nurrka, and DepositPhotos/prometeus

All rights reserved.

1st Print Edition. December 2020

ISBN-13: 9798580211930

FOR AUDIENCES 18+ ONLY

This book is intended for adults only. Spanking and other sexual activities represented in this book are fantasies only, intended for adults.

CHAPTER ONE

Kasia

"He's here!" Diana shuts my bedroom door and presses her back against it. Her cheeks are pale, her chest is rising and falling rapidly.

"Have you talked to him?" I scoot off my bed. She shakes her head; tears well up in her soft brown eyes.

"I can't." She covers her mouth.

I go to her, pull her into a hug. "Don't worry, Diana. We'll figure a way out of this. Dad can't do this; Mom won't let him." I pat her back while she winds her arms around my middle.

This isn't new. Me comforting my twin sister over something our father has done.

"He's already done it. Mr. Staszek is here too. They have a contract laid out on the desk. They're talking about this like I'm a prized cow." She lets go of me and runs her hands over her cheeks. Tears have stained her face.

"A contract?" My stomach turns. It's not real, it can't be. What judge would uphold an agreement like this?

"Yes." She walks across my room, twisting her hands together. "Mom's not even home. She left. She left me to do this on my own."

"That's not true." I defend. "If she's not here, it's because he made her leave."

Diana nods, rubbing her temple. "I know. I'm sorry, Kasia. I'm losing my mind here. This can't be happening. It just can't be."

She's in no state to go down there and deal with our father. With the Staszek men. Her hair is wound up in a tight bun and she's dressed in a soft blue romper.

"Has Dad seen you already?" I ask her as I make my way to my vanity.

"What? Yes. He's the one that told me they were here. I'm supposed to be waiting in the living room, but I had to come up here. I had to get away from it for a moment." Fat, fresh tears roll down her cheeks again.

"Okay, come here, get out of that romper." I sit at my vanity and pull out the pins needed to get my hair wound up like hers. I hate having my hair twisted up the way she does, but no choice for it now.

"Why?"

"Mr. Staszek won't know the difference. Give me your romper," I say urgently. If she's supposed to be waiting in the living room, it means they'll be calling her soon. We don't have much time to make the switch.

"This isn't second grade, Kasia. We can't do this." She rolls the romper over her hips as she argues with me.

I finish with the last pin and quickly change out of my t-shirt and leggings and into her outfit.

"You can't go down there sobbing. It will show weakness, and men like them, they feed off it," I say, repeating the words of our father.

She wipes her nose with the back of her hand. "Kasia. I'm the older one, I'm supposed to protect you, not the other way around."

I work the last button in place, then go back to my vanity to swipe on makeup. Diana favors blues; I dig out an eyeshadow pallet and get to work.

"You're older by six minutes," I say as I finish the last of my mascara. "Let me do this for you. I will deal with Dad and the Staszeks, and you stay up here. Out of sight." I squeeze her shoulders.

She sniffles. "Okay. Okay." She nods. "Thank you, Kasia."

I smile. "What are twins for?"

I leave her to hide away in my room and make my way quickly down to the living room. I'm just sitting down on the couch when Mr. Marcowski, Dad's new attorney, comes to fetch me.

With a cleansing breath, a quick mental prayer, I follow him down the hall to where my father is waiting.

I hate my father's office. It's never been a room that created any pleasant memories for me. This is no different.

"This must be Diana." An older man I assume is Joseph Staszek smiles at me. His face is squishy, like he's recently lost a lot of weight and his skin hasn't snapped back into place. He inclines his head in greeting but doesn't come toward me.

"Diana." My father says the name with contempt. The way he speaks my own name. He knows. To call me out on my trickery would embarrass him in front of these men, and he won't do that. But he'll deal with me later.

"Diana, this is Mr. Joseph Staszek. And this is Dominik Staszek, his son, your intended."

Intended. Sometimes I wonder if my father even understands the modern world. He's so entrenched with old rituals and rules; he sounds as outdated as the furniture in his office.

"Mr. Staszek." I force a smile for him. Diana is more civil than me, more polite. She wouldn't offend anyone in this room, and even with my father aware of the switch, I don't want to make her first impression to these men a bad one.

When I move my gaze to Dominik to greet him, a chill runs down my back. He's not my age. He looks well past high school years. His hair is cut on the long side, and his beard is well trimmed. It's his eyes that give me pause. Ice blue.

"Dominik," I say quietly and avert my gaze. He's dressed in a black suit with a regal blue shirt, no tie. His hands are tucked into his slacks, but even with his position I can see the muscles beneath his clothing.

"Diana." He inclines his head. "It's nice to meet you."

"The contract has been worked out; we only need your signature, then you can go up to your room. I know you have a lot of homework to get to," my father says. He's referring to the biology report I haven't completed. The tutor my mother made him hire is nothing more than a tattletale.

Mr. Marcowski walks to the desk and turns it toward me, holding out a pen for me. I swallow hard beneath the stare of all four of them on me. Diana would have crumbled in this room. She would have fallen into a fit of sobs. Being made to sign away your future can do that to a sixteen-year-old girl.

I glide across the room, my chin held high and snatch the pen from his hand. The attorney points to the last empty line at the bottom of the paper. Everyone else has already scribbled their names.

"You don't need to read it. Just sign," my father snaps at me. I clear my throat as a way to keep from commenting back, then put the pen to the paper.

Easily the pen glides over the paper as I scrawl my sister's name on the line. Signing away her future. Signing away any chance she had of falling in love the way a girl is supposed to.

"Good!" Mr. Staszek claps his hands together in celebration. He should be happy, from what I was able to glimpse of the contract his family stands to inherit all of my father's businesses upon his death. There is no son to pass the business onto, this is the next best thing.

"They will be happy, back home," Mr. Staszek says.

"This little feud—it's over," he says and waves over at Dominik. "Why don't you escort your bride for a few minutes."

Dominik gives a slight nod.

What feud are they talking about?

"Let's go, Diana." Dominik touches my arm when he gets close enough. The way he says the name, it's bitter. Is he as unhappy about this arrangement as Diana is?

"I'll be up to talk with you later," my father calls to me as we reach the door. I don't bother to acknowledge him. He can add it to the list of things he'll punish me for. I don't care.

Dominik towers over me as we walk down the hall.

"I can walk myself, thanks," I say to him as we get to the stairs. "I'm sure you have things to do."

He grabs my hand as I step onto the stairs and pulls me around to look down at him.

"You're not Diana," he accuses.

I school my features. "Why would you say that?"

"Because I saw Diana scurry like a scared mouse when we arrived. She wasn't wearing any earrings, and she was wearing white sandals." He gives a pointed look at the black flip flops. I forgot the shoes.

"Does it matter? You got what you came for. A signature," I say, pulling my hand from his. It's too big, too powerful. "How old are you?" If we're skirting small talk, I'd like some information.

"Twenty-five," he says with a grin. "You're sixteen. Don't worry, I won't claim your sister until after she's graduated high school. She's a free bird until then." He places one hand on the banister and leans on it. "Tell her, I expect her to be at the wedding. And if I were you, Kasia, I'd teach her a bit more about bravery. She's going to need it." He winks, then pushes away from the stairs, pockets his hands, and saunters back down the hall toward the office.

Whistling.

The asshole is whistling.

I run up the stairs to my room.

Two years. I have two years to find a way for my sister to get out of this marriage.

Because my sister will never survive being married to a man as cold as him.

CHAPTER TWO

Kasia

It's four in the morning when I arrive home. My feet throb from the insanely tight shoes I stuffed them into for the night. I'm going to have blisters for days. My eyelids are heavy, and all I want is my bed. I haven't stayed out this late in too long of a time. I may sleep the rest of the weekend away.

My father's driver pulls up to the front steps of the house, parking behind a black SUV. I don't recognize the car, but I'm too tired to really care.

A girl from school threw a graduation bash in the city at a dance club. It wasn't my scene. I don't go out often, rarely actually. Making friends isn't worth the hassle anymore. But her father knows mine, so it was more of a demand that I go instead of a suggestion for some fun.

Four years of college, and I'm still being bossed around by daddy. It's pathetic.

I carry my shoes with me up the steps to the house. The porch light's on and two of my father's men are standing at the door, waiting.

"Evening boys," I wink at them as I pass them into the

house. They don't smile. To show me any kindness would probably earn them a beatdown.

I can't blame them.

"Kasia." Mr. Marcowski steps out of my father's office further down the hallway. He doesn't move toward me, but rather beckons me toward him. "Your father would like you in his office."

"What's going on?" I ask. I just want to go to bed.

"Your father wants you," he repeats himself.

I've been out all night, doing what my father told me to do. How much trouble could I have caused him while doing exactly what he wanted from me?

"Is someone here?" I ask, noting two more men standing outside my father's office. They aren't his men. These two are younger, more severe looking. No, they're obviously not in their own territory.

My heart is already beating too fast in my chest. I steel my features. It's not much, but it's all I have. I take a cleansing breath and wipe my palms on my hips before walking into the office.

Whatever his problem is, I'll deal with like I always do. And then I'll move on.

Once inside the brightly lit study, I stop. Marcowski enters behind me and closes the door. The loud thud of it shakes my insides.

My father sits behind his massive desk, drumming his fingers on the arms of his chair. He hates waiting, and apparently, I'm late for a meeting I didn't know about.

Off to the right of my father stands a man. A familiar man.

Dominik Staszek.

My heart trips over itself when I recognize him. He's aged, but haven't we all. The years have made him fiercer, at least in appearance. Where he seemed serious before, he looks downright dangerous now.

His hands are stuffed into the pockets of his trousers. His hair is slicked back from his face. He scans my appearance, as though taking stock of me. How much have I changed in the six years we haven't seen each other? The years that I've almost forgotten about him.

There's no point for him anymore.

Not since the accident.

My throat dries as the tension in the room builds.

"Kasia." My father finally breaks the silence. "I thought you'd be home earlier." Anyone who doesn't know Marcin Garska would think he sounds casual, but I know my father. He's annoyed.

"I was downtown at the graduation party, like you...suggested. I didn't realize you needed me home at a specific time." My eyes wander from my father to the serious man still glaring at me. I avoid his pale eyes and try to assess him in the same manner he did me. He's wearing a dark gray suit with a black button-down shirt. No tie and the top button is undone. Every bit of his clothing fits him like it was made specifically for him.

"You remember Dominik Staszek." My father points to him but doesn't stand up. And Dominik makes no move toward me. No extended hand or a smile. Just a simple nod of acknowledgement.

I was never formally introduced to Dominik. Other than the meeting where I posed as my sister, I have never spoken to him. A sadness showers me with the memory.

I swallow hard. Something's out of sorts here. Diana isn't here. She was killed along with our mother in a horrible crash long before she was forced to join hands with him. Dominik shouldn't be here. He doesn't need to be here.

"Yes, I remember," I say, rolling my shoulders back and standing as tall as my spine will allow. Look determined, confident, no matter how much your insides are crumbling.

"Let's get to the matter at hand," my father announces. "The arrangement made with Joseph Staszek and his son Dominik stands."

"What? Why?" I ask, focusing my attention on my father. I can feel Dominik's stare on me, spreading warmth over my skin.

"It's what was decided," my father says.

"But…how? I mean, the arrangement was for—" I hesitate at her name. "Diana isn't here to keep to the arrangement." I tense my body, willing myself not to show how much her name still affects me.

"I'm well aware of that," my father snaps at me, and a heavy wave of guilt rushes over me. "But an agreement was made. You'll honor it." My father looks right into my eyes, not an ounce of empathy crossing over his features.

"It's been years, four years past the agreement," I say quickly. Surely that has to mean something. He broke the deal by not coming four years ago.

"You'll have to forgive me for not coming sooner." Dominik finally speaks, his voice low, controlled.

I glance at him, then refocus on my dad. If I ignore him, maybe he'll go away.

"This isn't making any sense. You told me if I stayed, if I went to college and did exactly as you instructed, I would be able to choose for myself. I've graduated. I'm free. You said I could move—"

"Enough!" My father's eyes widen with his outburst. His lips curl inward, and I can make out the vein in his neck throbbing. This conversation isn't appropriate in front of Dominik, but he's brought this on himself. He should have told me sooner. He should have given me a chance to talk to him in private about this.

I look to Dominik. The man appears utterly bored. He could be staring at paint dry for all I can see on his expression.

"I don't understand," I say softer, unable to tear my gaze away from Dominik.

"What's not to understand? You're marrying Dominik. Simple as that." My father taps his hands on his desk and gets to his feet. He's made his decision.

There's a sound behind me. I turn just as Marcowski opens the office doors. The meeting is over. I've been informed and now I'm to just accept it. I'm not supposed to ask questions.

But I have so many.

"Go upstairs and pack a bag. Enough for a week." My father points at the open door. "I'll have the rest of your things sent to you in a few days."

This gets my attention, and I face my father. "Bag? Why?" Although the sick feeling in my stomach tells me I already know the answer.

"You'll be staying with me until the ceremony." Dominik answers me but doesn't move toward me.

My head whirls. No. My entire life is spinning out of control.

"Why?"

"So many questions," he smiles, but it's not a kind, gentle smile. It feels like a warning. I'm asking too many questions.

"It's for your safety, Kasia," my father says, quieter. "Go. Pack a bag. You'll be leaving with Dominik. He's waited nearly all night for you. He shouldn't need to make a second trip to pick you up."

And that's it.

I've been dismissed. Not just from the meeting, but from my home. My life.

"Do you even know this man?" I ask my father. Everything I've done over the past four years was to earn my freedom. I went to the school he chose, I roomed with girls he hand-picked. I did everything because after graduation, I'd be free to move out, to start a new life on my own. And he's pulled the rug right out from beneath my feet. Not so much as a conversation, a warning. Just a simple command thrown at me like I'm nothing more than a foot soldier.

No. Less than a foot soldier.

This is my life.

My father's eyes narrow, but I don't care. I'll take whatever punishment he wants to dish out; I deserve to know what's happening to my own life.

"I know everything I need to know. Now, don't show Mr. Staszek what a rude girl you can be, go pack your bag." He flicks his hand toward the office doors. He's dismissed me off hand.

Our relationship has strained over the years since the accident. It's hard for him to look at me. I understand that, I look just like her, so much like mom, too. And my part in it, he's never forgiven me. It has to hurt, even for a man who values his work over his family. But this is beyond what he's done before. He's throwing me into the arms of a stranger.

Tears threaten, but I turn away before anyone can see. I force my expression to wipe clean of the fear, the sadness.

"Kasia." Dominik's voice stops me at the door.

I turn slightly, waiting for him to continue.

"It was nice seeing you again."

My jaw aches, I clench it so tightly.

I march up to my room. Anger shakes inside me, fear wraps a cold blanket around me. But I hold it in, I shove it down. Because there is no other option. This is my life; this is my duty.

Once safety inside my room, I look around. Nothing here is really mine. Everything can be taken away at a moment's notice, most of it has been either a punishment or a test.

I grab a bag from my closet and get to work.

There are no options for me. It's not new, but this feels different.

I've been released from the grasp of one monster, only to be thrown into the grips of another.

CHAPTER THREE

Dominik

"She'll come around," Marcin Garska assures me once his daughter has left the office. I wait until the patter of her bare feet have faded off into silence before I address him.

"I'm not worried about her," I tell him, moving my hands from my pockets.

"I warn you, she's a stubborn girl."

I raise an eyebrow. "She'll be fine," I say, but I don't sense any actual worry from him. He looks almost relieved to be rid of her, and if she's being hauled off to hell, which I'm sure he believes life married to a Staszek would be, all the better to him.

"I was surprised when your father called." He's trying to fill the space of time it's going to take his daughter to stuff a few outfits into a bag.

"Why's that?" I ask, picking up the photo frame on his desk. It's a picture of his family. When they were a family. Diana is sitting on Marcin's lap, smiling for the camera while her father wraps his arms around her middle. Kasia, stands between her parents, a forced smile on her lips.

"Well, I know he's having some issues—"

"Issues that this alliance will help clear up," I cut him off. He seems to think we don't know what sort of underhanded shit he's been pulling over the years. Greasing palms is just part of living in Chicago for men like us, but he's been doing more. He's the reason my father's living in Warsaw right now, hiding from the government. But Marcin thinks he's too smart to get caught.

"Yes, of course. My resources are yours. Now that we will be family, we help each other," he says, but bitterness lays beneath his words.

"He'll be happy to hear that." I put the photograph back on his desk. "Kasia has finished school, you said. What did she finish for?"

"A degree in teaching," he scoffs, like it's the worst profession someone could have. My own mother was a schoolteacher before she married my father. But a man like Marcin Garska doesn't appreciate actual work. He's taken over his family from his father, whereas my father created our strength. He brought the Staszek family name up from nothing. It's something to be admired, but not to a man like Marcin. To him, we aren't as skilled, not as powerful. But he's wrong.

"And did she pick her degree or did you?" I ask, but I already have an idea.

"I chose for her," he says while raising his chin. "It's what's best for her."

"To earn a degree doing a job you find disgusting?" I ask.

"She wanted to go to college. I let her." He actually thinks he was being generous.

Walking around his office, I spy another photograph. This time it's just him and the girls. They are smaller, much younger. Diana is laughing, sitting on Marcin's shoulders, while Kasia, stands beside him, tugging on his shirt.

My jaw clenches.

"How is your sister? Your brother?" Marcin asks. I turn from the bookshelf where the photo is kept.

"Both are fine." I don't want to talk about them. I don't want to talk to him at all. I check my watch.

"She'll be down soon," he promises.

"I could help her," I suggest.

"Christopher," Marcin calls toward the door. One of his men steps inside the office. "Get Kasia from her room. Dominik is ready to leave," he states firmly. I don't miss the bitter way he speaks her name.

While the man scampers off to fetch my fiancé, I turn to the attorney standing in the corner of the room. There's no need for him here, but Marcin insisted.

"You handle all of the Garska legal issues?" I ask him.

He clears his throat and nods. "Yes, well, I have associates that help from time to time."

"You'll be sending the agreement over then. Confirmation that the terms have been seen to?"

He flicks his gaze to Marcin, then back. Maybe I should wait while he fetches the documents now.

"I'll have them to you by the end of the day," he promises.

"Good."

"She's ready," Christopher returns, poking his head into the office.

I take a look at Marcin. A father should have some reaction to his only child being carted off in the middle of the night. He has none. A figure of stone watching me from behind his damn desk.

"We'll be going then. Do you want a moment alone with her?" I ask. Shouldn't a father say goodbye to his daughter? If my sister were in Kasia's place—I don't finish the thought. Joseph Staszek would never allow such an arrangement for his daughter.

"No. I'll speak to her tomorrow. Once she's settled." He pauses. "I don't want to keep you waiting any longer than you have," he adds. Maybe he senses his reaction isn't normal.

"I'll let you know when she's...settled," I say, marching

from the office.

Kasia stands at the foot of the staircase. One of my men already has her bag in his hands, waiting for my instructions. I wave him off, and he scurries out to the car to put her things away.

She's changed out of the too-tight dress that barely covered her ass into a pair of black yoga pants and a white t-shirt. The neckline has been torn out, so the shirt is angled. Her left shoulder sticks out. Her hair is loose around her shoulders, the long locks in thick waves. She's washed off the makeup. There's a subtle beauty to her. Natural. The dark lashes and red lipstick overshadowed it. She looks better this way.

"Ready?" I gesture toward the front door.

Her brown eyes widen a fraction. Did she think this was all a game? A bluff?

She casually glances down the hall to where her father is still inside his office. Disappointment crosses her features, but it's only a flicker. Quickly hidden behind a blank expression.

Oh, sweetheart, you can't hide from me that easily.

She raises her chin and marches out of the house. It's the walk of the condemned.

Accurate for the moment.

CHAPTER FOUR

Kasia

Dominik's house is outside the city limits, but he told me when he climbed into the SUV after me we have to make a quick stop .

There's a familiarity to the neighborhood as the driver turns off of Milwaukee Avenue onto a side street. I recognize the corner building from years ago.

"Something caught your eye?" he asks from beside me. I stiffen at the deep tenor of his voice.

"That building is familiar," I say, leaning back into my seat. My suitcase has been tucked into the back, but I hug my purse to my chest. Orange hues are peaking on the horizon. The sun will be up soon.

"You've been there?" he asks but doesn't turn to see which building I'm talking about.

"When I was little."

"You lived around here then?"

I eye him silently for a long moment. "So many questions," I say, throwing his words back at him. I may have been brought up to know my place, but that doesn't mean I can't push boundaries.

His mouth kicks up at the edges.

He leans closer to me. I can smell the musk of his cologne. It's not thick and suffocating like some men wear; it's manly, but subtle.

"Rule number one. I ask, you answer." He stares at me, those blue eyes of his could burn my skin.

I have no idea why I'm here, why he would want to make me marry him. And until I do, it's best to walk a cautious line.

"We did. Probably a few blocks from here. I was very little; I don't remember exactly."

"But you remember that building?"

"My mother took me there for Polish school on the weekends." I remember our house, but I don't tell him that. Walking down memory lane from such a carefree time in my life doesn't bring me joy. It's just a reminder of what was taken from me, from my mother.

"Polish school?" His eyebrows quirk upward. "Your parents didn't teach you to speak it?" From his accent, I can tell he's a native speaker.

"My mother didn't speak Polish, so it was hard. My father worked so much he was rarely home. I can understand better than I can speak it," I explain and look back out the window.

"Your mother's not Polish then?" he asks, but I get the sense he already knows. He doesn't strike me as a man who doesn't know everything before moving forward with a deal. And taking me as his wife is nothing but a business maneuver, I'm sure.

"She was. My grandfather migrated from Poland, but my grandmother grew up here in Chicago. They never taught her the language," I answer, not giving him more. I'm not in the mood to discuss my family history. "Are we almost at your house?" I ask, shifting the bag in my lap. My cell phone buzzes from the front pocket and I pull it out.

"No. We're making a quick stop then we'll head home. It's about a half hour drive once we get on the highway."

He leans further over to me as I swipe my phone alive. "Don't." He puts his hand over my screen. His touch is warm when he covers my hand with his.

I bring my gaze up to his. He's not looking at my phone, but at me.

"Don't what? It's just a girl from the party, making sure I got home all right."

"Not yet." He easily pulls my phone from my grip and tucks it inside his blazer.

"She's just a friend," I say, putting my hand out. I want my phone. I haven't done anything to warrant him taking it away. I haven't even fought this stupid notion of us getting married.

"I know that." He pulls his own phone out and taps away on the screen.

The car slows and then pulls to the side of the street, parking in front of a three-flat. A single light is on in the front window of the garden apartment. The driver gets out of the car and walks quietly to the building. Dominik continues his tapping on his damn phone. A shadow, then two, appear in the window, then within a minute later, the driver is back outside walking to the car, tucking a thick envelope into his jacket. The light goes out in the apartment.

"Did he have it?" Dominik asks without looking up from his phone when the driver gets back inside.

"Every penny."

"See." Dominik tucks his phone away. "With the right incentive, they find the money. Have Janusz bring the wife home. I want her back here within the hour," he orders and my mouth dries.

"You kidnapped someone's wife?" I ask before I can stop myself. Did I think him less capable of evil than my father? They live in the same world, work the same business, but I never saw anything of my father's work. He sheltered us from all of it. It's one of the few kindnesses he's paid me over the years.

Dominik ignores my question. "It's going to take a while

to get home. You can nap if you'd like. I'm sure you're tired from your party tonight," he says, looking out the window, away from me.

I curl my fingers into my palms, pressing my nails into my skin. It hurts, burns, but it floods me with relief. This pain I understand, and I welcome it.

Over the next half hour, I stare out my window at the streetlamps along the highway. The sun is climbing back into the sky and by the time we turn off the exit, the streetlights have all gone to sleep.

The front gates of Dominik's estate open as soon as the car pulls up. After a short drive up a winding driveway, the car pulls up to a large American foursquare house. Flowers bloom in the garden along the front of the house and more in planters hang off the wooden deck. I expected something more…severe looking.

His door is opened by the driver and he steps out, standing to the side and offering his hand to me. I look from his hand to the house. It's beautiful. More inviting than the all-brick bungalow that my father lives in, but I don't let the contrasts in architecture trick me. I'm only moving from one prison to another. And this one has a locked gate around it.

I slide across the back seat and climb out of the car, ignoring his hand. There's no need to pretend manners.

Dominik wraps his hand around my upper arm and leads me forward up the steps. Once inside the house, Dominik is greeted by a similar looking man. He's a little shorter than Dominik, but his arrogance is just as loud.

"Jakub, you didn't have to wait," Dominik says.

"I didn't think you'd be this late," Jakub says, giving me a cursory glance then moving back to Dominik.

"It's been a night." Dominik drops his hand from my arm. The driver of the car brings in my suitcase and Dominik gestures toward the stairs. "Put those in the room next to mine. She'll stay there for the time being."

My own room. I suppose I should be grateful, but there's

still a sense of dread bubbling in my stomach. Everything has happened so quickly; I'm only now beginning to fully grasp my situation.

I don't know Dominik. Who is he to my father and why did he do this? I have no idea what's to become of me once this all plays out.

"Kasia, this is my brother." He turns to Jakub. "Jakub, this is Kasia Garska." Dominik places his hand on the small of my back. A gesture of ownership, I think, with the way he pulls me closer to him.

I extend my hand toward Jakub. "It's nice to meet you," I say. Not because I mean it, but because I'm acting on autopilot.

I need to get alone. I need to work all of this out in my mind.

Jakub's hand is gentler than Dominik's, but just as large. This man is as dangerous, I can feel it in my bones.

"Same here, Kasia. It will be nice to have some beauty in this house." He grins at me, but his gaze flickers to Dominik. Seeking his approval maybe. My father never cared for attention paid my mother so long as it made his business easier.

A flash of a memory hits me, but within a blink it's gone.

Dominik brushes his hand over mine, taking me from Jakub's grip. "Kasia, go up to your room and wait for me. I'll be there shortly." He gestures behind me, and the man from earlier is back. He's my escort. Or my prison guard.

"Wait for you?" I yank my hand free from him. My level of patience has reached its limit. I've been sold, then traded, and now I'm to heel like some dog and wait for my master to come to my room? It's too much.

Dominik must sense it, because he turns to me, blocking Jakub's view of me. He knuckles my chin up until my eyes line with his. There are those cold, blue eyes again, peering down at me like I'm nothing more than an object to be bought. His possession now, I suppose. I wonder how much my ticket price was.

"Don't cause trouble, Kasia. Go on upstairs and I'll come soon. I know you have questions, but not until we're in private." He softens his hand, cupping my cheek and running his thumb along my cheek bone.

"I'd like my phone back," I say quietly, matching him. He obviously doesn't want Jakub to hear our conversation, and I have no need for a witness either.

"I already said not yet. Don't ask me again, Kasia. I'm being patient, but don't take that as a weakness."

"Patient?" My eyes widen with my question. He can't be serious.

He doesn't respond with words, only caresses my cheek again before dropping his hand. There's a tingle where his touch was.

"Go on," he says with a flick of his head. A signal, I suppose, that I've been dismissed.

When I don't move, he leans in, his warm breath washing over my cheek.

"Rule number two. Always do as you're told," he whispers in my ear.

"As soon as I have my phone." I raise my chin, fist my hands at my sides.

His eyebrows raise. I think I've surprised him. I went so willingly with him from my father's home. I obeyed my father's instructions so easily, so quickly. Dominik probably thought he'd bought himself a nice doormat for a wife.

But I'm tired and done with all of this chest beating.

"Tommy, take her up to her room." Dominik gives the order without moving his gaze from mine.

Two strong hands wrap around my arms, and I'm pulled backward, then dragged toward the stairs. I try to yank free, but he's too strong, too determined to be the perfect soldier for his boss.

I give up on struggling and Tommy lets me go so I can walk up the stairs easier. Once we're upstairs, he grabs my elbow and pulls me down the corridor to a closed door.

"This is your room." He pushes the door open,

dropping his hand. His eyes are on me though, ready if I try to bolt. Where would I go? I doubt my father would let me go home, and without my phone I can't exactly order an uber to come save me.

I walk past Tommy into the room. The door shuts softly behind me and I'm alone. The enormity of the evening crashes on me. I'm in a room, in a strange house with a strange man who is bound to me.

Dropping my bag onto the floor, I sink into an armchair in the corner. I'm sure the room is lovely, but I close my eyes and suck in a trembling breath.

Who exactly is Dominik Staszek, and why does he want me?

CHAPTER FIVE

Dominik

Kasia is asleep when I go up to her room several hours later. She's lying on her side with one arm tucked beneath her head and the other tucked between her knees. She didn't climb under the covers; I wonder if she's chilled. Maybe she didn't intend to fall asleep.

After getting rid of Jakub, I had a phone call from my father. There's a good chance he'll be able to come home soon. The case built against him is mostly bullshit, and once the right wheels are greased to turn the other way on any legit issue, he'll be on the first plane home. Not that he's hating all his time lounging poolside at our family home in Pruszków. He's been wanting to visit the family estate for a long time. His legal troubles were a good excuse.

Kasia looks different today than the first time I saw her. Older, of course, but also more refined. Her hair is softer, her makeup more subdued.

I suppose I should feel bad. This unsuspecting girl isn't anything more than a means to an end. But when I look at her, sleeping so peacefully, I don't have anything like remorse. She had touted to Marcin he'd promised her freedom, but men like Marcin never let go of what they think is theirs. If he forced her to stay, to live the life he laid out for her, there would be no escaping it.

I won't play the hypocrite. I'm cruel, too, but not in the same way as him. Innocence matters to me. Well, it did until now. Kasia isn't her father, I know that. She doesn't deserve what's coming her way.

But there's no stopping the train now that it's left the station.

It's tempting to her let her sleep away the afternoon and talk with her tomorrow. I open the blinds, allowing the soft summer sunlight to wash over her face. It's enough to have woken me if I were sleeping, but she doesn't stir. There's a thick curl of hair covering her cheek; I brush it away. Still, she doesn't stir.

Does she trust her surroundings enough to fall so deeply asleep? Or has she always slept like the dead? I know nothing about this woman, other than what I've been able to dig up—which wasn't much. I know her father has magically kept her separated from his business dealings. She attended a private high school, then went to the University of Chicago where she received a bachelor's degree in elementary education.

Everything else about her though is a mystery. It won't matter. There's time to find out, if I have the need.

"Kasia," I say her name roughly, shaking her shoulder gently at first, then harder when she remains lost to sleep.

She jumps away, whipping her hand up from her knees to ward off an attack. Sitting upright, she scrambles across the bed to the other side, blinking as she tries to bring the room into focus.

"I didn't mean to scare you," I say, holding out my hands. "You were sleeping hard."

She rubs the heels of her hands into her eyes. "I'm sorry. I didn't mean to fall asleep." When she drops her hands, her mascara is smeared beneath her eyes. It's not much, a shadow at best. She'd been up all night, of course she fell asleep.

"I hadn't intended to be so long coming up." I straighten and slide my hands into my pockets. I've changed out of my suit and am wearing a pair of loose-fitting slacks and a black button-down long-sleeved shirt. Her gaze wanders over me, like she's looking for something.

"Why am I here?" she asks, folding her legs behind her and crawling backward off the bed. Now that the queen-sized bed is between us, she's found some bravery.

"I think your father made that pretty clear," I say, keeping my eyes locked on her.

"Marriage, yeah, I know. But why am I here now? Why couldn't I stay home until the wedding?" she pushes.

"It's safer here." My actions will come with consequences. But as much as I don't want her to have to pay for them, I also don't want my enemies to use her against me.

Her shoulders drop and for a second, I think she's going to let it go. She should let it go. Too many questions can be dangerous.

"Why is it safer here?" She emphasizes the first word. I don't miss how her hands fist at her sides, gathering the material of her shirt.

There's a little pink starting to tint her high cheekbones. There's fire there, beneath the surface.

"It's enough that it is." I dismiss her question without answering it. "It's important that you understand a few things."

"It's not enough that you say it is." She cuts me off. Her eyes widen. Does her outburst surprise even her?

"Kasia—"

"No. I deserve to know. I may not get a say in where my father sends me, or who he sells me to, but I deserve to at least know why it's dangerous for me to be at my own home." Her heart must be hammering in her chest; I can see the pulsation in her neck.

She's not wrong. But I can't tolerate her tone.

"Kasia, I understand this is all confusing and new and a little scary. But don't raise your voice to me," I say, putting my finger up when she looks ready to launch again. "It's better that you're here now. This is your home now," I say.

"Why?" she asks me, but she's not asking about where she'll be living now. She wants to know why she's engaged to me. Why I wanted her.

"It serves my purpose." I won't lie to her. I won't always tell her everything she wants to know, but I won't lie.

"And what purpose could I possibly serve?" she asks, her voice dropping. Her irritation is building again. "The agreement between your father and mine was for my sister. It's way past the time you were supposed to take her." She pauses, a flicker of pain flashes but disappears. "Were you not able to buy another bride? You had to circle back to my family?"

"Kasia, I'm trying to be patient today because I'm sure this is all overwhelming. But if you keep this up, raising your voice, I'm not going to be able to let it go for long." I stalk around the bed, keeping my gaze locked with hers while I make way to where she's standing. I'm a little surprised, and even a bit impressed, when the heat in her stare doesn't die as I approach. I expected her to cower, but instead, she looks ready to battle.

"Patient? Do you have any idea how messed up this is?" She raises her chin. "I'm not a thing to be bought." I think she's told herself that over and over again, but this is the first time she's allowed herself to give voice to it.

"One." I raise a finger in the air, pressing it to her chin. "I didn't buy you. Maybe that's something your father does, buys and sells women, but not me. So, I don't want to hear you say that again," I say.

She steels her expression too quickly for me to get a real sense of her reaction.

"How did you get my father to agree to this, then?" She doesn't know details, but I think she knows more about the world her feather lives in than he told me. She's smart.

"You don't need to know about that." I move my finger from her chin, up along her cheek, gathering her thick hair and tucking it behind her ear. There are pearl teardrops dangling delicately from her earlobes. These aren't costume jewelry. They're real. Expensive, too, with the diamond studs.

"Of course not." She pulls away from my touch. Her tone sours. Maybe the nap wasn't good for her. She's woken up with a vengeance.

"What you need to know right now, Kasia, is we're going to be married."

Her gaze shoots away from me. "And then what?" she asks, her shoulders slumping. It's a logical question. And I don't have an answer for her.

"Then we're married," I say, keeping it simple.

A low rumble escapes from her stomach.

I smile. "Margaret made food for us. It's in the kitchen, let's get you something to eat."

"Who's Margaret?" she asks.

"My housekeeper." I move to the door and open it, gesturing her to come with me. She's not a prisoner. Not exactly. Her movements will have to be restricted for a while, but it's for her safety. She'll understand that.

Or not.

Either way, that's how it will be.

She eyes the bed momentarily. Her options are to stay hungry and in her room, or deal with having me for a dinner partner. Her hand presses to her stomach, and I'm certain hunger has won out.

She keeps her back rod-straight as she brushes past me and heads down the hall to the stairs. Her movements are confident, strong.

It's just dinner, but she looks like she's headed into battle.

A fight she will never win.

Ever.

CHAPTER SIX

Kasia

Dominik's kitchen is gorgeous. The entire house is beautiful. Modern, sleek design with a lot of open space. It's warm, a house I can imagine children running around playing. It's a direct contrast to what I see when I look at him.

He's large, forbidding, cold. Even with the change out of his suit to more casual shirt and slacks, he appears all business. And well rested. Did he sleep before coming to get me?

As soon as I sit at the built-in breakfast nook in the corner of the kitchen overlooking the backyard, his phone rings. He pulls it out of the back pocket of his pants and looks at it. With a frown he answers the call and steps further away from me. I can't understand him, but I hear how fast he's talking. He's not happy.

"Oh, good, you've come down to eat," a woman probably in her sixties says, popping out from what I think is a pantry. She smiles brightly at me and offers her hands. I reach out to her and she grasps both my hands in hers and shakes them. It's more of a hug than a handshake, and she looks genuinely happy to see me, so I don't pull away until she lets me go.

"Forgive me," she says, swishing her hand through the air. "I'm Margaret. I'm Mr. Staszek's housekeeper. There are two other women who also work the house, cleaning, laundry, that sort of thing, but if you ever need anything just come straight to me and I'll see it done," she tells me. "There's pork chops, mashed potatoes, and green beans all set for you and Mr. Staszek." She looks around the kitchen, maybe she expected him.

"He had a call," I tell her, and she nods.

"I'll fix you a plate then."

"You don't have to, I can—"

"No, no you sit. I'll get it. You must have had quite the day," she says and there's a comfort with her acknowledgement. Quite a day is the understatement of the year, of my life.

I thank her when she places the plate she's made up for me in front of me. It's a heavy meal for the afternoon, but having slept all day, I'm starved.

Dominik is still in the other room. He's keeping his voice down, but I see him pacing the living room.

Margaret puts a second place on the table for Dominik along with silverware and an opened bottle of beer. She offers me wine, but I only want water. I just want to eat and go back to my room.

"Do you live here too?" I ask. The house is so large, too large for just one man to live in.

She smiles. "No, but it feels like it some days." She gestures to the plate. "Go on and eat. Sometimes his calls last a while. Is there anything else I can get you?"

"No, no. Thank you." I pick up my fork and knife, ready to dive into the pork chops. She's breaded them and the smell makes my mouth water.

"I'm going to check a few things and then I'll be heading home. But if you need me, my number is on the inside of the pantry door or let Mr. Staszek know and he'll call me."

She adds the last part like she just remembered I'm not allowed communication with the outside world.

I thank her again and cut into the pork chop. A shadow behind the blinds startles me. I must have made a noise because Dominik hurries back into the kitchen.

He ends his call. Pressing one knee into the bench, he leans toward the window to check out what spooked me.

"It's just my men," he says to me, then knocks on the window and gestures for whoever it is to move. "Smoking," he explains and sits down across from me, looking at my plate.

"You have men surrounding the house?" I ask. The estate is gated, and from what I saw of the neighborhood it's not exactly slum living.

"More than your father, but you'll get used to them," he explains and cuts into his own meal.

He chews a bite of pork while staring at me across the table. It's like he's assessing me still. Maybe I'll come up short and he'll send me home.

I begin eating, not asking any more questions. It's better I stay ignorant, I think. Let him have his life and I'll find a way to have mine. This won't be a real marriage, so we don't need to pretend it is. Two separate people living in one house. It's large enough, we probably won't see each other very much anyway.

"You sleep like the dead," he says after I put my fork and knife down.

"I was tired. And it's not like there's anything else to do up there." I've always been a heavy sleeper. It takes two alarms to wake me up in the mornings.

"There's a tv room downstairs in the basement," he tells me and takes a pull of his beer.

"I'm not going to be locked away in my room?" I ask, surprised.

"Not unless you need to be," he answers with narrowed eyes. "Do I need to lock you in your room? Are you going to be a naughty girl and try to run away?" He cocks his head to the side, studying me.

I force my expression to go blank. At least I hope I do. I can never tell if I've mastered the art or if I'm as transparent as I feel.

"When can I have my phone back?"

He takes another sip of his beer. "We'll see."

"We'll see?" I can't stop the anger boiling up. "You just said I'm not to be locked away."

"You aren't. You're free to roam the house and even the grounds, but you aren't to leave the property and you aren't to speak to anyone until I say so." He pushes his plate away and stands up from the table.

I scoot out of the nook. "What if I say no?" My heart jackhammers in my chest. This man kidnapped a woman yesterday, what will he do if I piss him off too much? But I don't want to walk around on eggshells. I'm tired of it. I'm so tired of trying to placate those around me for fear of making a splash.

"Say no?" he asks, leaning one hip against the kitchen island.

"If I don't agree to marry you?"

His eyes narrow to thin slits, but it doesn't keep the heat from his glare hidden.

"Because I don't want this. I don't want to marry you."

In three steps he's in front of me, the toes of his expensive leather shoes pressed against the tips of my ballerina flats. He pinches my chin between his fingers in a hard grip and pushes my head back until I have to look down my nose to see him. Moving closer, he looms over me.

"Do you have a boyfriend? Someone you're in love with?"

His question throws me for a moment. "No," I answer when I recover.

His eyes roam over my face, more inspections. I'm not a liar, but I'm not sure he's ever known anyone in his life that didn't lie to him.

"Then we'll work fine together," he says, running the flat of his thumb over my bottom lip. The part of me that should be screaming at my legs to move, to carry me away from this dangerous man isn't working. All that's registering is the warmth of his touch, and how the pain of his grip is sending electric waves through my body, straight to my center.

"I don't want to marry you," I say firmly.

"We don't always get the luxury of only doing what we want," he says, shifting his hand to cradle the side of my face. His thumb traces my cheekbone. "You'll be a good girl for me, Kasia. If you don't... If you try to refuse me..." He leans closer to me, the tip of his nose pressing to my ear. "You'll be punished like a bad, bad girl."

I curl my fingers inward. This man could break me if he wanted to.

His mouth presses against my cheek, then my chin, finally he covers my mouth with his. It's not tender, his kiss. It's a branding. He's marking me. I try to blank out, to just let it happen, but he won't let me.

He grips the back of my neck, holds me to him and deepens the kiss. I want to fight him off, to push him away, punch him, kick at him, because despite what I want my insides to do, I'm melting beneath him. Maybe it's the power, or the ownership he's trying to convey.

When he pulls back, it's with an arrogant grin. He knows what his touch is capable of doing. And I'm just another victim.

He must know I want to get away from him, because he fists his hand in my hair, holding me steady.

"You can look at me with all the hatred you want, Kasia, but you can't hide the reaction your body has to my touch."

"It's just a physical reaction, nothing more." I'm not telling the whole truth though. I've been kissed before. This is different. This left a tingle on my lips, and a wetness in my panties.

"I want to go back upstairs," I say with gritted teeth.

"There's that word again. *Want.*" His lips pull up into a wide, toothy smile.

"You're an asshole," I say hard, shoving at his chest. He still has my hair and he grips it even harder, twisting a little until I grimace at the sharp pain shooting through my scalp.

"Such a dirty mouth." He turns away from me, walking me back to the breakfast nook where our plates still sit.

"Dominik," I say reaching behind myself and smacking at his hands. "Stop it. You're hurting me."

"You wanted to play tough, Kasia, calling me an asshole. Not a great start to our relationship." He's mocking me. I hate him for it.

"You are an asshole, now let me go!" I demand. I have zero leverage here, but still I force myself to be strong. I know what he thinks of me, of what my father has told him. Kasia's an obedient little thing. She'll just lie down and take whatever you dish out.

"Again, she says it!" He laughs, but there's no joy there. No levity.

Dominik plants his left foot on the bench of the nook and turns a heated glare on me. "Say it again and I'll turn you over my knee and show you what happens to naughty girls in my house."

This night has taken a turn I didn't expect. How did I find myself here? Why can't I stop myself, why do I push him?

"You. are. An. Asshole. Dominik Staszek. A fucking asshole." I enunciate each word. I've lost my mind. There is no other explanation.

He smiles at me, like he's pleased. Like I just made his day with my proclamation.

"I like strong women, Kasia," he says, then tips me over his leg. I'm dangling upside down, my butt high in the air on his knee. I scramble to find purchase on the floor, but I can't touch. My hands don't reach either.

"Let me go!" I yell, swinging my hands at his calves.

"I like strength, but I expect respect and obedience. At

all times," he informs me and before I can register his words, his hand makes contact with my ass. I stiffen at the first impact, almost unsure of what's happening. Another and another smack of his hand and I'm fully aware. Warmth spreads over my cheek. He's concentrating on one spot, spanking over and over again.

I kick, but it does me no good.

"Stop!" I say, ramming my fist into his calf.

He pauses, and I take a deep breath. It's over.

But it's not. He yanks my leggings down beneath my cheeks. Cool air touches my bare skin.

"Not much protection back here," he says and tugs the thin material of my panties up until they bunch between my cheeks. The bikini panties don't cover much, but they're more comfortable than thongs.

"Dominik. Stop. Please," I say in a calmer voice.

"You made a choice, Kasia. Now you pay the price," he says and lays into me again. He doesn't discriminate this time and peppers both ass cheeks with hot spanks. I squirm and fight, but in the end, all I can do is give over.

My ass burns, the heat spreads throughout my entire body.

He stops spanking me, but rests his hand on my ass to keep me where I am. Tears have built in my eyes, but I've managed to keep myself from breaking into sobs. He won't get that from me.

Dominik rubs some of the sting away with his hand. It's a gentle touch, throwing me off again. Is he a monster or not?

Seconds tick by with nothing being said, then he tips me back to my feet. My panties are still stuffed between my cheeks, and I leave them there. I won't dig out the wedgie he gave me with him staring at me.

"Did you learn your lesson?" he asks. I expect gloating, but he's being sincere. His tone is soft.

"You don't like cursing," I say, managing to keep the snark from my tone. I don't want to repeat the lesson. I just want to go to my room and let the humiliation kill me in privacy.

He runs his hands over my hair. "No, Kasia. I don't like disrespect. You're an adult, if you want to curse go ahead. But you won't be disrespectful." He stands back and tucks his hands into his pockets. "You can go to your room now if you want." He nods toward the front of the house.

It strikes me then. All the lights are on in the house. The curtains were open in the living room before. They're closed now. Someone came in while he was spanking me and closed them.

A new wave of embarrassment rushes over me. Did his men out back see? There are no curtains on the windows here. They were out there smoking earlier; did they watch my humiliation?

"Kasia."

I blink and move my attention back to him.

"My men know better than to watch things that don't concern them," he says quietly. How does he understand my thoughts so easily? "Go on if you want. Or go downstairs and pick a movie." He shakes his wrist and looks at his watch, a large piece of machinery. Not one of those high-tech watches, but an actual wristwatch. "I have some business to deal with tonight."

I've been dismissed.

I nod in silence, unsure of what I will say if I open my mouth. Will I rage at him for touching me in such a way? Or will I kowtow to him? Either would be horrible. I yank my leggings back up in one quick tug and hurry away from him.

"And Kasia," he says as I reach the next room.

I turn halfway so he knows I'm listening.

"No touching yourself tonight. You get no pleasure on nights I have to discipline you."

Mortification sets in and I calmly make my way to the stairs. Step by step I get further away from him. Hot tears roll down my cheeks and I'm glad I'm already upstairs before they start to fall.

Don't touch myself?

Once back in my room, I sit on the edge of the bed. How did he know how what he did affected me?

Everywhere I turn there's an enemy. Even when I look in the mirror.

My body betrays me.

I open my bag and change into a pair of pajama shorts and a tank top. Catching a glimpse of my bare ass in the mirror, I sigh. It's red, but not as bad as I thought it would be.

After I throw my hair up into a bun, I climb under the thick covers of the bed. I wipe away tears. I won't cry because of this. I just won't. This is my home now, my bedroom, my life.

No, this may be where I live, but I'll never call this my home.

CHAPTER SEVEN

Kasia

The house is quiet in the morning. When I slip downstairs, it's empty.

"Good morning!" Margaret greets me when I enter the kitchen. She has a large smile and a plate of pancakes and sausage for me.

"Is Dominik here?" I ask, settling into the breakfast nook. The home of my humiliation. Does Margaret know what he did to me? Would she have stopped him if she'd seen?

"No. He left an hour ago. He'll be back for dinner, though." She puts a small pitcher with warmed maple syrup on the table.

What am I supposed to do all day alone in this house? At home I had my computer, my phone, my life.

"I think I'll go to the bookstore if there's one around here. Is there a car I can use, or can someone—"

"That's not a good idea." Margaret shakes her head and goes to the sink. Of course, he would tell her I'm not allowed to leave. I'm not a prisoner, but I can't go anywhere.

I finish my breakfast and bring my plate and silverware

to Margaret.

"I can help you today," I offer.

Again, she shakes her head. "No, no. I have all this handled." There's a beeping sound and she scurries off to the iPad on the counter. After a few swipes there's a live feed from outside playing. "Ah, looks like the men are back with your things."

"My things?" I slept later than I'd hoped to, but it's still morning. How early had they gone to pick up my belongings?

Two men carry in boxes and go upstairs. Apparently, they know where I'm sleeping. People are having conversations about me behind my back, it's unsettling.

After the last box is brought up, I go up, too.

"One of the girls should be here soon, I'll send her up to help." Margaret says from behind me.

There're three boxes in all. My entire life fits into three boxes.

"No, that's fine. Thank you, but it's mostly clothes. I can do it. It will give me something to do."

She gives me a small smile then leaves me to it.

It's nearly all clothes. Nothing in my father's house was ever really mine. I'm happy to find my laptop and my tablet, though. I have a full library on my tablet. If nothing else, I'll be able to put a small dent in my reading list.

After I've hung everything in the closet and put away everything else in the dressers, I sit in an armchair that faces the window. The backyard is large and sectioned off with fruit trees. A row of pine trees lines the back wall of the estate.

Would it be hard to climb over the wall? More importantly, where would I even go?

"Kasia." The door to the room opens and Dominik walks in.

"Can't you knock?" I say, turning back toward the window. I thought I'd have a longer reprieve from him today. It's barely afternoon. Shouldn't he be working, shaking someone down or something?

"Knock in my own house? No," he says firmly and stands beside the chair. "I brought you this, but if you're in a mood I can keep it a bit longer."

My phone is in his hand. I look up at him. No smile, just a raised eyebrow. I take it from him.

"Thank you," I say quietly.

Has he done anything to it? Put some sort of tracking app on it? Can he see who I talk to, who I text?

"I spoke with your father. He has to go out of town for a while, but he'll call you this afternoon." He slips his hands into his pockets. He's wearing another suit. A black suit and tie set against a dark grey shirt. With his hair slicked back, and his beard neatly trimmed, he looks more like a handsome businessman than the demonic thug I'm sure he is.

My phone's dead; it needs a good charge.

"How long will he be gone?" I ask. The longer he's out of town, the longer the engagement. I'll have time to think of a way out of this or get Dominik to change his mind.

I get up from the chair in search of my charging cable. It was among my tablet and computer.

"A few weeks at best. He mentioned you recently graduated. Did you have plans, a job offer maybe?"

I had a lot of plans. A lot of things I wanted to do next. Getting married to a mob boss wasn't one of them.

"Kasia, I asked a question," he says when I keep quiet.

After I dig out the cable, I turn to him. "Does it matter? Would you change any of this if I did?"

"No." He answers without a second of hesitation and I have no doubt he wouldn't have thought twice about his actions if I had a full life of achievements and goals ahead of me. My life means nothing to him. Not when he can use me for whatever purpose he has in mind.

I shake my head and go about plugging the charger into the wall.

"Then why bother asking?" I mutter.

He doesn't answer me, but instead walks to the empty boxes.

"You're unpacked all ready? Where are the other boxes?" he asks.

"That's all there was."

He goes to the closet and flips through my things.

"What are you doing?" I demand, standing at the doorway.

"Your father was supposed to send all of your things," he says, looking annoyed.

"He did," I tell him.

He looks back at the clothes but doesn't make another comment. Did he think I was a prized possession that had been spoiled with baubles since childhood? He'd be sorely mistaken. Everything given was at risk of being taken. My father didn't raise his hand to me, not once. He found more satisfaction in taking things away. He took away my toys as a child, kept me from my sister as punishment, and when there was nothing tangible to take anymore, he took away my freedom. Things and people can be taken away; it's better not to have them in the first place.

"I'm glad you don't have any more dresses like the one you were wearing the other night," he comments, pulling a sun dress from the rod and looking it over.

"It was an old dress. It didn't fit right. I don't go out that often to need club clothes," I explain, snatching my clothing from him and putting it back on the rack. "I don't usually wear things like that."

He studies me for a long minute. Like I'm not what he thought I was. Though how he could have any sort of opinion about me in the past few days is beyond me.

Though I have a damn good assessment of him.

"Good." He steps closer to me, brushing my hair from my shoulders. "How is your ass today?"

His question throws me off balance. Before I can stop it, heat rushes to my cheeks, and I'm sure I've turned red right before his eyes.

"I'm not talking about that with you," I say and leave him in the closet.

"Should I look for myself?" he asks, right on my heels.

Spinning around to face him, I bump into his chest. With a rumble of laughter from his chest, he catches me and puts me at an arm's length away. I hate how easily he handles me. How much my skin tingles with excitement when he lets go. I felt nothing when other men have touched me, but this man brushes against me, and I feel like a firecracker ready to go off.

He grins. "Maybe I should."

"I'm fine," I answer quickly.

"No. I think I should check." He tilts his head, like this is a dare. Do I obey him, or do I fight him? He stands a full head taller than me, and his muscular build suggests he could benchpress two of me without breaking a sweat. I'd never win in a physical fight with him.

"I already answered you," I say.

"Are you afraid if I look, if I touch you again, you'll get as excited as you were last night?"

"I'm not afraid of you." I stalk across the room and check my phone. There's enough of a charge I can shoot out a text message.

"Maybe not." He's behind me as I start typing. His hands rest on my shoulders, and he presses his chest into my back. If he's trying to scare me, it's not working. I should be afraid. All common sense points in that direction, but I can't summon the fear. Maybe I've finally lost all sense and simply don't care how I meet my end.

"You may not be afraid of me, but you're definitely scared of your reaction to me." He brushes his lips across the shell of my ear. I freeze, my thumbs hover over the touchscreen of my phone.

"I need to call my friend. She might be worried since I didn't answer her the other night," I say, letting all the bitterness saturate my words. He deserves them. He's earned it.

"Have you been spanked before last night? And I mean a real spanking, not a little tap from your father's hand as a child." He lets go of my shoulders and moves to the window, briefly looking down at the yard below before bringing his attention back on me.

"I don't want to talk about this." I close my eyes, willing him to leave. It wasn't enough to humiliate me last night; he wants to relive the embarrassment. I won't play along with his games.

"It's a question, Kasia. How did your father punish you, as a child, as a teenager, as the woman you are now? Tell me." He presses the issue. He's like a dog with a bone; he's not letting go.

I text Trina that I'm fine, I'll call her later, and drop the phone back to the table.

"He didn't hit me. No one has ever done what you did last night." I stand straighter. I won't show weakness now. "And I won't allow you to ever do it again."

"Allow?" He laughs on the word. "That's not the way this works, and you know it."

He's right. I do know. I'm to obey. Do as I'm told. I live in the modern age, but my life is stuck in the traditions of the past.

"Now answer me."

Why does he want to know this so badly?

"Parents punish their children." I'm not even close to answering him, but I feel like staying away from the topic of my father with him.

"They do. But how did your father choose to do it?" he asks.

"He took my things from me," I answer with a roll of my eyes. It sounds so silly saying it out loud. "Are you happy now?" I don't tell him of the punishments when I was younger. When Diana was still alive. That my father would tear us apart and not allow us to see each other as punishment. Sometimes it would last weeks, once it went on for over a month.

"Is that why you don't have anything?" He looks around the room. Other than my electronics and a small jewelry box, I've added nothing to the room. "There's nothing here but your clothes and some jewelry."

"Nothing in my room at my father's house was really mine."

He studies me for a moment. The sun is already setting outside, and an orange cast falls over his face.

"What do you want from all this, Dominik?" I ask when he seems content to stay silent. "Why would you want me to marry you? What do you gain? What did you give my father to get him to agree to this?" I'm being used as a pawn; shouldn't I get to at least know the prize for the game?

His smile falters a fraction and he open his mouth like he's going to speak. He must think better of it, though because he snaps it shut and shakes his head.

"Dinner will be ready soon. I'll be out all night. Margaret can get you anything you need." He steps away from the window and points to my phone. "Do not make me regret letting you have this back so soon."

I stare at him, unable to understand him. Why won't he give me an answer to anything?

He quietly leaves my room and shuts the door, drowning me in the emptiness once again.

· · · · · · ·

My father's supposed to be out of town, and he never calls me when he's left the area. Work takes up too much of his time. So I'm surprised when my phone rings and it's him.

"Kasia, I only have a minute. I need you to listen to me," he starts off right away, not even saying hello.

"Hi to you, too, dad. I'm fine, thanks for asking. It's not like—"

"I don't have time for your whining. Listen to me." He cuts me off. There's something different in his tone. He's agitated but more, he's worried. "I only allowed him to take you that night because I need you to watch him. I need you to listen to his conversations, find out what you can about his father. Find out when he's coming back from Poland. Find out about his associates, who he works with, who he takes meetings with."

"What are you talking about?" I ask, looking out my bedroom window. A gardener is watering a rose garden. So much beauty in such a dark place.

"His father. Dammit, Kasia, listen," he barks at me. "You need to find out when his father is coming back from Poland. As soon as you know, you call me. Don't talk to anyone but me. Do you understand?"

"Don't you have men for that sort of thing?" I ask. Dominik isn't going to confide anything in me.

"I need to know when and I need you to find out who Dominik is talking with. Names of anyone who comes to the house, who he has meetings with."

"Why would he tell me anything like that?"

"Make him. Get him to trust you and then find out what you can."

"Why? What's going on?"

"Do as you're told for once, Kasia!" His voice raises and I pull my phone from my ear slightly. "Diana would have it done by now. She wouldn't ask so many damn questions all the time."

My heart sinks into my stomach.

"But she's not here, is she, Kasia?" Poison drips from his question.

"No. She's not," I say quietly. I may be outspoken. I may have walked on the edge of what was proper, but he can reel me back in with merely mentioning my sister. My mother.

The guilt guts me, and he uses it to his advantage whenever he wants.

"I'll see what I can find out," I promise him. I gave up a long time ago that he would find a way to forgive me, but still, a small part of me believes he might. Maybe if he does, I might be able to find forgiveness for myself too.

"See that you do. And don't let him know you're poking around. He's a dangerous man, Kasia."

The call disconnects and he's gone.

I hadn't heard from him since he sent me off in the dark of the night with Dominik, and when I do, it's this. He wants me to be a spy.

How the hell am I supposed to do that?

And what will Dominik do to me if he catches me?

CHAPTER EIGHT

Dominik

The drive from the city to home takes longer than normal, but I'm happy for the silence. With my father still overseas with my sister, everything is left on my shoulders. It's good practice for when my father turns over the family to me, but I'll be grateful for the day he's back home and his legal troubles are over.

I know Marcin is behind the bullshit keeping my family stuck in Poland, but until I can find the information I need I won't get the okay to act. The marriage between Diana and me was supposed to put an old rivalry to bed, but her death changed things. Without the tie, the old men back home allowed Marcin to move into my father's territory.

It's taken me five years, but I've built up our own business to recover the loss. But it's meant nothing but work over the years.

"Has Kasia been inside all day?" I ask Tommy. He's driving me home, but he spent all day at the house. I wouldn't put it past Marcin to make some move to take her home, to help her escape the future. The ceremony needs to happen soon. Once we have the certificate, once our marriage is finalized, her father can't make any more moves on my family. And when I find the evidence I need that he's behind my father's indictment, the old men back home will grant us what's ours.

"She went out to the garden for a bit to sit with a book. But that's it," he informs me.

I nod but don't ask any further questions. I text Margaret to tell her to hold dinner until I'm home. I'll make Kasia have dinner with me tonight. I let her sneak away to her room yesterday, but there won't be any more of that.

The house is quiet when I walk inside. Margaret meets me at the door, her hands wringing in front of her.

"What's wrong?" I ask her, looking toward the staircase. Kasia is behind her frown, I can feel it in my bones.

"Kasia is in your office," she tells me.

"What is she doing in there?" I ask, Margaret wouldn't stop Kasia from wandering the house. I never gave her instructions to keep Kasia away from my office.

"I don't know." The wringing of her hands gets harder. "She locked the door."

The key to the room is in my pocket.

"Okay, I'll talk with her."

"Dinner is ready."

"Just put it on the stove," I say and take off toward my office. Someone needs a lesson in being nosey. She may or may not be going to bed without dinner. It depends on her answers to my questions.

When I come to the door, I stare at it for a moment, listening. Something drops, then a curse. I pull the key from my pocket and slowly slip it into the lock. I want the element of surprise here. I want to see what she's up to without giving her enough time to hide her actions.

With a quick turn of the lock and flip of the handle, I step inside. She has her nose buried in my laptop. But her hands freeze over the keyboard.

"Kasia," I say her name tentatively. I'm not sure if I should be angry with her yet.

"Dominik," she mimics my tone. Strike one, little girl.

"What are you doing in here?" I ask, walking around the furniture and behind where she sits. I grab the computer before she can close it.

"Nothing." She sits back in my chair and folds her arms over her chest. "Am I not allowed an internet connection?"

I pick up the laptop. She's checking email. The inbox is empty, mostly newsletters and advertisements. This is a decoy email. I wonder what's in her actual account. The one she uses for real correspondence.

Closing the laptop, I set it aside on my desk. I'll have someone go through it to find out exactly what she was doing in here.

"You have internet up in your room," I remind her, pushing the chair around until she has to look up at me.

"I thought I'd just sit in here. I mean if this is to be my home, I didn't think any room would be off limits." She tilts her head. "Or is it?"

There's a challenge in her eyes. She's been caught doing something she shouldn't be, but she's daring me to call her out on it.

"You locked the door. Margaret was worried." I put one hand on the arm of the chair and another on the desk. She's sweetly caged before me.

"Why? I'm in the house. Locked away just like you wanted." She lifts a shoulder. A lot of sass for a girl who's been caught snooping.

"What were you looking for?" I ask, knowing full well I can't trust her answer.

"I told you, I was checking email."

"You want to stick to that?" I ask, giving her a chance to come clean.

Her bottom lip tucks back. She's trying so hard to stand her ground, to keep her secrets. With my thumb, I pull it free and run my thumb along her lip.

"I wasn't doing anything wrong," she says finally. She believes the statement, that much is clear. So, either she was doing something she thinks is right, but I would disagree, or she was doing nothing. The pink hue on her cheeks suggests it's the first. She's guilty, but she's trying to convince herself otherwise.

"Rule number three, Kasia. No lying to me. Ever."

Her jaw tightens. She hates my rules, hates that I give them to her and expect her to be obedient to them. It's fine, she can hate them, despise them, but she will follow them.

"I'm not lying," she says with hesitation, like she's testing out the words, unsure if they'll stick.

"I heard something drop before I came in. What was it?" I ask, keeping my eyes trained on hers.

She gives herself away too easily, flicking her gaze for a fleeting second to the ledger on the bookcase next to us. It's a worthless book, filled with made up numbers and contacts. Fiction for the feds if they should ever find reason to go through my things. There's nothing in this house for them to find, or her for that matter. Whatever she was looking for, she won't find it in here.

I push off the chair and pick up the ledger.

"This?"

"It fell. I picked it up and put it away," she explains quickly. For having such a corrupt father, she never learned the art of deception.

Her innocence combined with the building fear in her eyes makes my cock stir in my slacks. She's dressed in a summer dress today, a light purple cotton dress. Her long thick hair is braided down her back, but a few strands won't be tamed and frame her face. She's to be my wife in a matter of days, being attracted to her is only a bonus.

"It just fell over on its own?" I ask with a raised brow. "That's an odd thing for a heavy book like this to do, don't you think?"

She's holding her ground. No matter how caught she is, she's trying to find a way out. Since there's no real harm done, I could just let her leave. Let her go hide back in her room. But I'm not a good guy. I never claimed to be, and I never will.

"Stand up, Kasia," I say, snapping the book closed and shoving it back on the shelf.

"I'll stay out of your damn office, Dominik," she says and shoves out the chair, making a break for the door.

I stop her easily enough with one arm wrapped around her middle.

"Where you going, sweetheart?" I ask on a chuckle. "We're just talking." I pull her back to me.

"Dominik. Let me go," she says, smacking my hands.

"No," I say, holding her to me tighter and forcing her to walk across the room to the wall. With a shove, I pin her to the wall with one hand pressed between her shoulder blades.

"I hate you. I really fucking hate you," she says, struggling to push back against me.

"That's okay. But what's not okay is snooping in my office and lying about it." I move closer to her, pressing my chest against her back. My cock is steel hard and I can tell the moment she feels it pushed against her ass. She freezes. It's only for a second, but it's there.

"I was just…" She doesn't even finish the lie.

"You want to know about me? About who I am?" I whisper in her ear. Fuck, she smells like vanilla and lilacs. It shouldn't make a difference, but it makes my need for her become even greater. As much as I like the scent, I want my own on her. I want her to wear me like a brand.

"I know who you are." She shoves back again. I'll give her credit, she's a fighter. "You're a fucking monster."

I grab hold of her braid and pull her head back until I'm able to look into those dark brown eyes.

"You think your father's any different? You think any man he married you off to would be kinder? I haven't touched you since you got here. A lesser man would have already taken what's his." I'm not sure why I say this. It's not relevant, but somehow, I need her to know I've shown restraint. As much as I've wanted to sink myself between her thighs since seeing her bare ass that first night, I've held back. I vowed to myself I'd leave her untouched until we were married. But fuck if she isn't making it hard to keep that promise.

Her struggles cease and she stares up at me, waiting for what comes next.

"I told you on the first night, I won't tolerate disrespect. I don't take it from my men, I won't allow it in my house." I press her head to the wall, not hard enough to hurt her. That's not my goal. At least not for that part of her.

"Leave me alone. Just let me go upstairs." She starts up again.

I grab hold of the buckle on my belt and with one hand undo it. The jangle of the buckle catches her attention, and she freezes.

"Dominik. Dominik, no!"

"Are you going to tell me the truth yet?" I ask, whipping the belt from the loops of my pants. "What were you looking for in here?"

Her hands are fisted against the wall, her fingers tucked tightly.

"I…nothing. I wasn't looking for anything," she says, sealing her fate. "Please," she says the word so softly, it barely registers.

"I've given you plenty of chances to tell the truth." I say, letting go of her back. "Pull up your dress," I order.

She shakes her head but says nothing.

"If I have to do it for you, I will bind your hands and your feet, and you won't get just a few licks of my belt. Now pick up your dress. I want your bare ass to taste the leather."

After a moment, she rolls her shoulders back, stands straight and bunches the skirt of her dress up in her hands. The white bikini underwear is thin, it won't offer any protection, but that's not the point. With one hand I grab the elastic band and yank the material down to her knees. She shuffles forward a step from the force of my actions, but she rights herself quickly.

"Now lean forward." I give her shoulder a gentle push.

"Still don't want to come clean? Still want to be a little liar?"

"I can't," she whispers.

"You can. Your loyalty is to me now, Kasia. Only to me," I tell her, adjusting my stance. I don't want the belt to wrap around her hip, only to strike her ass, so I wrap it around my hand until it's the right length. The buckle is tucked in my palm.

"No?" I ask, staring at her profile. Tears are in her eyes, I can see them, but she's holding them back. She's steeling herself for what's coming. I know she wasn't snooping for her own knowledge. Her father's behind it, all she has to do is tell me. Just be honest, and I won't have to paint her ass red.

But she's stubborn. Marcin warned me about that.

"When you tell me, the spanking stops." I condemn her and bring the belt down across her milky white cheeks. She hisses but makes no other sound. Again, I bring it down, crossing over the red mark of the first lash. I pause, giving her a moment to say something.

With a bitter shake of my head, I continue. Again, and again, I spank her ass with my belt. Watching her plump cheeks bounce after each strike. I give her time, I give her chances, but she remains silent other than to utter a curse between swats.

"Fuck!" she screams when I hit the same spot twice in a row.

"Tell me, Kasia. This doesn't end until you're honest."

I drop the belt to the floor and move closer to her side. With one arm around her belly, I pull her to my hip. Her ass is in prime position. It's red, a few purple marks are already showing. I won't give her much more, but she still has to obey. She will not get away from telling me the truth.

"Please." She gasps for air but I'm not listening to anything other than the truth. In my gut I already know, but I need to hear the words. I need to know she's not following her father's orders anymore, that she'll be following mine. I can't let my own wife be my enemy. Not when this isn't her war.

"So be it," I say and bring my open palm down on her ass. She wiggles a bit but once I get into a steady pattern, she stops moving. She's crying softly, but she's not fighting me. She's not giving in either.

When I move the spanks to her thighs, she sucks in some air, but melts into me. Fucking hell, she's soaring. I stop, look at her eyes and confirm what I already know. Her eyes are glossed over; her bottom lip is swollen from her biting it so hard.

I'd set out to punish her, to teach her to obey, never lie to me, and what I've done is set her skyrocketing off into subspace.

Well, fuck.

CHAPTER NINE

Kasia

My ass is on fire, and the quilt on my bed isn't making it better. I roll to my side, fluttering my eyes open to find Dominik sitting in the armchair beside my bed. His eyes are set on me, the cold blue unrelenting. His jaw, tight.

He was spanking me. Embarrassment floods me. It had hurt so bad, so fucking much, but within a few stripes of his belt it had turned into something else entirely. Something that surprised me but was welcomed.

I don't remember him stopping or being carried up to bed, but I'm here. He must have brought me.

My dress is still on, but my panties are gone. There's a distinct wetness between my thighs.

Can human beings actually burst into flames from humiliation?

"You're up," he says to me when I stay quiet. What am I supposed to say?

I start to sit up, but he puts his hand out. A signal to stay put.

"Obviously, an ass whipping won't get through to you," he says with a sadistic smile. "How do you feel?" His question throws me for a second. It's what he does best, drags me one way then tosses me the other.

"I'm okay." I don't elaborate. My ass is sore, and my mind is a little fuzzy, but all in all I'm peachy.

Why am I so relaxed?

"Good." He leans forward, his elbows pressed into his knees and his hands dangling between his legs. He's holding something, but I can't tear my gaze away from him to look. Whatever it is, I'll deal with it.

"Do you know what this is?" he asks, putting the device in my line of vision. It's a vibrator. He's holding a goddamn vibrator.

"I do," I say, feeling the hot rush to my face.

"There are other ways to punish, Kasia. Spanking won't work with you, and we will explore that later, once I have your obedience and your loyalty. But pleasure can be punishment too." He gets up from the chair and moves to the bed. There's enough space for him to sit beside me. When I try to curl up, to roll away, he places his heavy hand on my stomach, stilling me.

He grabs the hem of my dress and flicks it upward until I'm exposed. I fling my hands down, trying to cover myself, but he brushes them away.

"No, Kasia. Bad girl," he says and rests his hand over the small patch of curls. "Keep your hands to yourself." He pulls my left leg toward him then shoves my other leg away. I'm open, exposed, and too shocked to do much else but obey.

"You're…" the insult forming in my brain dies away when he spanks his hand over my pussy.

"I would watch my mouth if I were you right now, Kasia," he warns, curling his fingers into my pubic hairs. With a little tug, he has my attention. "I like this little patch. Don't shave it. Keep it just like this for me," he instructs me, and I want to scream at him, but I can't deny the urges boiling inside me either.

"What do you want?"

He quirks an eyebrow. "The same thing I wanted downstairs. I want the truth. What were you looking for and why?"

"I was just using the office." I try to sound sincere, but by the look of disappointment on his face I've failed.

"Have it your way," he says and flips on the vibrator. The humming sound fills the room right away, and my clit reacts to it immediately. Vibrators are not new to me.

Using two fingers on one hand, he spreads my pussy lips open. The tip of the vibrator touches my clit, just barely, just enough to make my body react. I fist the bedding beneath me. I can't give in to him. I can't let him win.

He presses the vibrator harder against me, and it takes every ounce of energy I have not to buck up at it. I want it, I want it harder and faster and I want to come unglued.

"It's nice, right? Having your pussy played with," he says softly, leaning over until his hot breath washes over my clit. He moves the vibrator lower, until it teases my entrance. "Tell me," he says looking up the length of my body at me.

Those eyes, these fucking eyes bore into me.

I grit my teeth and turn away. If I don't look it will be easier.

Wrong.

His tongue touches my clit, rolls around it and then he sucks it into his warm mouth while he pushes the vibrator just inside my pussy.

I moan, clench my teeth. It's coming, this buildup of pleasure is mounting and mounting and he's not stopping. He's slowly fucking me with the vibrator while he licks and sucks on my clit.

I'm at the very edge, ready to leap off into an abyss of pleasure, when it all stops.

"No!"

He laughs. "Didn't like that?"

How badly would he hurt me if I slapped him?

"Tell me."

"There's nothing to tell," I say from behind clenched

teeth.

"Okay," he says and the pleasure ramps up again. The vibrator goes deeper. His tongue flicks faster. Everything is ten times what it was a moment ago. I tense, letting it build, hoping it will all crash down on me before he can notice.

But I'm wrong.

"Tell me," he says again from between my thighs.

"You already know!" I accuse him. This man doesn't act without knowledge. He knows damn well what I was doing and why.

"I do. So just tell me," he says with a wide grin.

I turn my gaze up to the ceiling and it all starts again. Only this time, he's not fucking me with the vibrator. He's using it on full power on my clit and I'm driven straight to the very end of sanity. It's too much, everything is going to burst. I can't do it again; I can't be so close to heaven only to see it fade into the distance.

"My dad!" I yell. It's all I can say. He already knows, he just needs my confirmation.

"Good girl," he whispers.

I'm so close, so fucking close. The very first ripple of an orgasm is right there.

And everything falls away. All the pleasure, the buildup. It recedes, leaving an agitating hum behind it as it fades away.

"You said," I whine. I hate that he makes me sound this way, but I'm desperate and needy and horribly embarrassed.

He shoves the vibrator into his back pocket, pulls my dress back down over my pussy and climbs off the bed.

"I never said you'd get to come. I said pleasure could be punishment. And it is." He wipes the back of his hand across his mouth, where my own juices have wet his lips. Mortification will kill me in this house.

I snap my legs together, pressing them tightly.

"You, you…" Words fail me. My brain is broken.

He laughs. "Be careful. The punishment can continue."

I sit up in the bed, pushing myself against the headboard.

I want to scratch out his eyes. So easily he'd brought me to the edge. It's not fair. It's wrong.

My stomach aches at my actions.

"You can spend the rest of the night up here. Think about how you'll be more honest in the future." He winks then heads to the door. "Just to be sure you don't go stealing what's not yours, the door stays open tonight. One of my men will be sitting just outside to be sure you're safe."

"You're a horrible man," I say quietly. I don't trust myself to say anything else. Tears burn my eyes, but not because I'm left unsated, but because I wanted nothing more than for him to make me come. I wanted his touch, I ached for it. I betrayed myself. And now he knows my father wanted me to find information.

I've betrayed him, too.

"I can be, yes," he agrees, his hand on the handle of the door. "I don't want to be, not with you. But that's up to you, Kasia."

He leaves the door open as he promised, and one of his men walks past the door and sits in a chair. I see his knee bobbing up and down from where I am.

Punished and put to bed.

Will the rest of my life be like this?

CHAPTER TEN

Dominik

Kasia is lost in a book beneath the weeping willow in the yard. She's settled herself into a lawn chair that had been dragged into the shade. There are no tread marks in the grass.

"Did you bring this out here by yourself?" I interrupt her reading as soon as I'm in her earshot.

She looks up from her kindle, shading her eyes with her hand.

"No. One of your big, strong men did it for me."

She's trying to goad me into an argument, but it won't work. Not at the moment. We have more important things to discuss.

"There's an umbrella on the patio, you don't have to come all the way over here to sit in the shade."

"I like sitting under the trees or in the rose garden. But there's less shade there though, until after lunch." I'm surprised by how much she says. It's been all two or three word answers so far.

Tommy shows up with another chair in hand and places it beside me. Margaret at his side.

"Here's your tea, Kasia." Margaret waits for Tommy to put the small folding table down beside her then puts down a steaming cup of tea.

"I would have come in for it…" Kasia sits up straighter in her chair. "Thank you."

"It's no trouble at all. Tommy was looking bored anyway." Margaret gives me a quick glance. "Would you like something while you're out here?"

"No. Thank you," I say with a small nod.

"I don't mean to be any trouble," Kasia tells me when the pair have walked away.

"Making a cup of tea isn't any trouble. I'm sure she's glad for someone to do things for." I sit down in the chair Tommy brought out for me, and stare at her for a moment. She's brushed her hair out and swept it into a side ponytail. The soft pink sundress she's wearing is a modern cut with a low neckline, but not low enough to show me much more than the curve of her breasts.

She must sense me staring at her, and tugs down the hem of her dress. It's a modest dress, even with it hiked up a bit with her legs crossed she's not giving me a glimpse at anything. After last night I don't need to see what she has between those sweet thighs of hers. I can still taste her on my tongue.

"Did you close my bedroom door last night?" she asks.

I bring my eyes up to hers. "Yes. When I went to bed, I checked in on you then closed it." She'd burrowed herself so far under the quilt, I had to go up to the bed to be sure it was her hair poking out and not some makeshift dummy. The woman sleeps too heavily. The house could have burned down around her, and she wouldn't have noticed.

"Thank you." She scratches her calf. "For closing it."

I nod. I didn't think she was thanking me for the spanking. But now that we're on that subject.

"How are you today?" I ask, wiggling my finger at her bottom.

Her cheeks redden in a single heartbeat. "I'm fine."

"Come here, Kasia," I say, sitting back in the iron patio chair and crook my finger.

"Not out here, Dominik. Please," she says quietly, frantically looking over my shoulder.

"I told you, my men know better than to watch what's not their business. Now come here."

She puts her kindle down on the table beside her tea and unfolds her legs. Once on her feet she shuffles the three steps toward me. Prisoners look less concerned while being marched to the execution room.

I spread my legs, capturing her between them. With a twirl of my finger, I direct her. Her jaw tightens, but she does what she's told and spins away from me.

Since she can't see me, I take a moment to enjoy the curve of her hips. Tenderly, I touch my fingertips to her legs where the hem of her dress touches. I drag my hands upward, pulling the material with me. Her hands twitch at her sides, but she's being a good girl for me and not fighting me. Maybe she did learn a lesson last night.

I think she learned something about herself, too.

"No panties?" I ask, somewhat surprised, but then I see the marks. There're two long welts crossing both cheeks that would make sitting uncomfortable. A dark purple bruise sits right where her panties would hit.

"Are you done?" she asks, her hands fisted, and she sounds close to the edge.

"I have some cream that might help," I say, poking the welt. She hisses and takes a small step forward. My cock is pressing hard against the zipper of my pants. I grab her hips, pulling her ass toward me. She stumbles back a half step, but I'm holding her, she won't fall.

I run my tongue over the largest welt then press my lips to the purple flesh where she probably likely hurts the most. Her ass tenses, but I'm not done. I created each of these marks, and I'll show them the respect, the care, they deserve.

"Dominik." Her voice is soft, more of a caress than a plea. "Don't, please."

"These are mine, Kasia," I tell her in Polish. "You're mine." I kiss the last welt.

I'm sure she understood me; her legs locked up when I made my claim.

"We'll be married by the end of the week," I say, pulling her down into my lap. Her bare ass hits my thigh. She winces.

"So soon?" she asks, trying to scramble off. I lock my arm around her waist and shake my head. I don't want her to go yet, and with the pressure on her ass reminding her of what happens to naughty girls, she stays put.

"Sooner if I can manage it," I say, brushing the tip of my nose against her bare shoulder. The dress has thick straps, but the rest of her is exposed. Creamy and untouched by the sun.

"I don't want this, Dominik. Doesn't that mean something?" She folds her hands in her lap and keeps her attention focused on the grass beneath my feet. Her bare feet dangle between my legs. It's cute the way she fits in my lap so snugly, so perfectly. Like she was made to be right here.

"Things will be awkward at first. But you'll get used to me. And I'll get used to you." I might be lying, but not with intent.

"And what you did last night. Will I get used to that too?" There's a sharpness to her tone, but she softens it by keeping her face turned away from me. I think she's embarrassed. Something new happened to her last night, and she doesn't understand it.

"Which part, Kasia? The part where my belt made you feel so good you couldn't speak? Or when I punished you by withholding your orgasm?" I scrape my top teeth across the curve of her shoulder. She folds her arms over her stomach, like moving that fraction of an inch will protect her from the sensations I'm giving her. She's not wearing panties and her ass is on my leg. Her pussy is already wet, making a mess on my pants.

"Both were punishments in my mind," she says, finally turning her gaze to me. Her pupils are dilated, nearly overpowering the brown of her eyes.

"Ah, the first was meant to be a punishment. I was hard on you with my belt, but what you experienced wasn't a punishment. Have you felt like that before?"

She bites down on her lip, and she quickly turns away from me again. Not before I see the red tint to her cheeks though.

"It's called subspace. Sort of feels relaxing and tense all at once, right? Like you were there, but not really?" A few women in my past have explained it that way.

She lowers her chin, like she's trying to fold herself into herself.

With a knuckle beneath her chin, I nudge her gaze up to meet mine. "There's nothing to be ashamed of. Nothing to be embarrassed about," I assure her.

"It hurt like hell and then it…" She swallows. "Then it didn't. It's like I heard you, I felt it, but I wasn't really there."

I run my thumb along her jaw. "You like the pain. It's good." I don't mention how much I enjoy giving it to her.

"Since you think I enjoyed it, you won't do it again?" There's a test in there somewhere. Does she want me to say yes or no?

"It won't be punishment, that's for sure," I laugh.

"The other part then, you'll… do that?" She's soft in my arms like this. The tension has eased away enough that I loosen my grip around her waist.

"Definitely." It's a vow. "I think it worked well, don't you? You're being more cooperative today."

She pinches her lips together and for a moment I'm sure she's going to argue with me.

"Don't you have work to do?" she asks, tugging her dress down. It's too late, her pussy has left a mess on my leg.

I lean forward and pull her phone from my back pocket. She looks at it with furrowed eyebrows.

"You took my phone?"

"Your father is blocked. I don't want you contacting him."

"Because I was in your office." She takes the phone and swipes through the contacts. He's been removed, but I'm sure she knows his number.

"Because he asked you to spy on me. He asked you to do his dirty work for him. I don't want you put in the middle of this, so I don't want you talking with him until it's all sorted out."

"He's my father..." The fire in her words dies quickly.

"Tell me about your sister." I sit back against the cushions of the chair and run my fingertips up and down her arm. I don't want to talk about her father any more than she does; a distraction from the topic will make it easier for her to open up.

"I don't like talking about them," she says, looking at me through a side glance.

"My mother died when I was in high school," I tell her. "She was sick for a long time. When she died, my sister, Lena, was only seven. My brother twelve. I was sixteen. She was alone when she passed. We were all at school and my father was away from the house for the day. The nurse was in the next room, getting my mother a glass of water. When she came back into the room...she was gone." I haven't spoken of that day in years. But seeing the pain in Kasia's eyes at the mention of her sister and mother, it's drawn out of me.

"I...I didn't realize your mother was gone," she says quietly, slightly turning on my lap to see me better. Her thigh brushes my cock, and even with the turn in topic, I want her.

"When I got home, when I found out she'd died alone, I blamed myself. I was the oldest. I should have stayed home when my father couldn't be there. I should have been with her."

"You couldn't have known," she says quickly. When our

eyes meet, her shoulders drop.

"I didn't like talking about her for a long time because the guilt would hit me hard when I did." I rub my hand up and down her back. "But you're right. I couldn't have known. She suffered a brain aneurism. It was a shock, even with her being so sick."

She looks away from my eyes, settling on the top button of my shirt. "It was my fault my mom and Diana were in that accident," she announces firmly.

"How so?"

"My father told me to pick up my mother from a luncheon she was having at a friend's house. I was in the middle of a project for school, and Diana was running out to get a new bottle of nail polish, so she offered to do it for me. I should have told her no. I should have done what my father told me to do."

Tears well up in her eyes, and I realize just how strong she is. Through everything that's happened in the past few days, she hasn't shown one crack in her armor. But now, talking about her sister and her mother and the guilt she carries, it's there. A hairline fracture, but it's there.

"And you think if you had gone there wouldn't have been an accident?" I finish for her.

"There wouldn't have been. Diana picked mom up early so they could go to the store together. If I had gone, we would have been at that intersection later. Or not at all."

"There's a lot of weight on that if," I say, pressing my lips to her shoulder. "The night I signed the agreement with your father, when you pretended to be Diana. Why didn't she come down?"

Now that I have more information, I pull her away from the topic bringing her pain. I don't like seeing the sadness in her. I fucking hate it, actually.

"She was scared. She couldn't stop crying, so I told her I'd go for her." She blinks a few times and looks away again, probably gathering up her strength again.

"You were her protector," I say softly, then tap her

phone. "Let me protect you right now. Stay away from your father."

She sighs. It's not a new idea that her father is a son of a bitch. He's probably been laying on the guilt ever since the accident. From the pictures in his office, it was plain that Diana was his favorite. Did anyone give Kasia the attention she needed? Or is that why she's built such a strong spine? Out of need to protect her sister and also herself.

"He's not a horrible man, Dominik. He's just...a hard man." She doesn't sound convinced, but I'm not going to argue with her.

"Did you disobey me last night?" I ask her, throwing her off topic again. She's easier to deal with when she doesn't see things coming. She drops her guard for a brief moment, and in that moment, I see her more clearly.

"For fuck's sake, Dominik," she admonishes me.

"That's not an answer," I say, resting my left hand on her thigh.

"No, I didn't do what you thought I was going to do," she says in a harsh whisper.

I laugh. "There's no one here but us, and I already told you — my men know better than to watch what's not their business."

I run my hand up her thigh, until my fingertips are just beneath her dress. "Since you were good and since you're being so cooperative today...let me make you feel good." I press her back into my chest and push her thighs open.

"Dominik." She tries to argue, but my fingers are already working over her pussy.

"Such a wet girl."

She groans, out of embarrassment or pleasure? We'll see.

CHAPTER ELEVEN

Kasia

I roll my head back, against his shoulder. The wind makes the tree branches dance above us, and I try to concentrate on them, on anything that will distract me from the easy way he arouses me. It's not right, to have no feelings for a man but still melt into his touch so effortlessly.

He presses a finger to my clit, the magic button that steals a moan from me. It only makes him more arrogant; these sounds he forces from me. Sliding his finger through my wet sex, he toys with my entrance, and it takes everything in me not to snap my legs shut. To keep him away or to trap him, I'm not sure anymore.

"Such a good girl when your pussy's being played with, hmmm?" He teases me with his whispers in my ear. The heat of his breath, the aroma of his aftershave all work together to make me want him even more.

I clench my teeth. This isn't right.

"Don't." He warns me with a light tap to my thigh. "Relax your body, Kasia. Let me make you feel good." He nips my earlobe. "Let me show you how good things can be between us. And they can be so good."

I can't stop the images from the whipping from replaying in my mind while his fingers rub over my aching clit. I wanted nothing more last night than to explode in his hands, and quickly he's bringing me right back to the edge.

Dominik's chin presses into my shoulder while he pulls the front of my dress down. The neckline is elastic and easily maneuvers beneath my breasts.

"No bra?" he asks, and I don't need to see him to know he's smiling. That same arrogant grin.

My nipples harden beneath his stare before he even touches me. But when he does, when his fingers gently pinch my nipple, it's like skyrockets are lit, firing between nerve endings.

"You're close, Kasia," he whispers in my ear. I nod, unsure of what I will say if I try to speak. I won't beg him to let me finish. I won't plead for my release.

"Such a good girl," he kisses the side of my neck, trailing a line of heat with his tongue. "Tell me, Kasia. Are you a virgin?" His finger slips just into my pussy. It's not enough, I want all of it.

"Dominik." One word. My cheeks flame with the truth. A twenty-two-year-old who's never known the real touch of a man, it's pathetic.

"Tell me, Kasia. Do I have to find men to kill or will I be the first man to have you, the only man to have you," he says, biting down on my shoulder. The pain of his bite burns at first, then mingles with the pleasure his fingers are giving me.

He pushes his finger inside further, curling it at the knuckle.

"Are you a virgin?" he asks again, his finger stilling inside me, his pinch increasing on my nipple.

I can't help but arch my body until my hips thrust toward his hand.

"Yes," I say. The heat from my cheeks spreads throughout my entire body.

With one quick thrust, he plows his finger into me, then

adds another. I wrap my hand around his forearm, squeezing him. I don't want him to stop. No, if he stops, I'll find his gun and kill him myself.

"You're so tight, so fucking wet," he mutters in my ear, biting my shoulder again and pinching my nipple.

I'm at the end, there's nowhere to go but over and once I breach that cliff, I'm not going to be able to stop myself. I roll my head to the side, giving him better access to my throat. Wanting, no, needing his bite, his marking as the heel of his hand hits my clit.

"Come for me, Kasia. Show me you're my good girl, you're my sweet girl. Show me," he says and plows his fingers harder into me, curling them and twisting as he fucks me with them. My nipple burns when he releases it, only to flick it and ignite another sensory overload.

All the pain, the pleasure, it's too much. I can't stop it. I can't contain it.

He licks my neck, then bites down hard, catapulting me beyond reason. The heel of his hand presses harder against my clit, rubbing in circles. The sounds of his fingers pumping in and out of my sloppy wet pussy carry me away. Every muscle in my body tenses and within a blink of an eye, I'm screaming. My feet plant onto the soft ground below and I'm scrambling to chase after every wave, every pulse of the electric release he's brought down on me.

"No, no," he soothes me. "Feel it, feel all over it," he commands, and like the good girl he's making me be, I sink into his lap, letting every harsh wave crash over me and steal away my breath.

By the time the pleasure fades into a lavender haze, I'm gasping for air. My heart has tried to escape my chest, but failed, leaving behind an ache as my pulse slows. His fingers never left my passage, his hand never moved from my breast. There's a light sting on my neck where his teeth sank in. I wonder if there's any blood.

I'm not sure I care.

He slowly pulls his hand from between my legs, leaving

me empty and wanting. After he licks his fingers clean, which I'm oddly aware of because of his moan, he rights the neckline of my dress and pulls my legs across his. I'm cradled in his lap now, and I don't even fight the urge to weave my arms around his neck and hold onto him.

He smells good. A masculine scent of spice and leather.

"This is how I want things between us, Kasia. Giving you pleasure, making you mine. This is how it should be between husband and wife."

"But we don't even like each other," I say into his shirt.

His chest rumbles with his soft laugh.

"We don't hate each other. And that's a start." He pulls me tighter against him.

"You want something." I'm sleepy, but I can tell there's a command coming. Another of his rules.

He kisses the top of my head. "I don't want you talking with your father. I want you to stay away from him." He's already told me this.

"You don't trust him," I say on a yawn. I don't trust my father either. A man who signs away both of his daughters with as much ease as he did, isn't a man with much integrity.

But he is my father.

"No." He surprises me by being honest. "I don't. And until I know what he's up to, I want you away from him."

His chest muscles tense. Here comes the bombshell.

"We're going to be married tonight, Kasia."

No matter my exhaustion, I push away from him to stare into his eyes.

"Tonight?" There's no time to plan. I don't have a dress, there's no guest lists, no parties.

"We'll throw a celebratory party once my father returns home. You'll plan it all the way you want it, but we need to marry. We need to get it done before your father makes whatever move he's planning."

I blink. Sleep is fogging my thinking. "But he signed that agreement. He can't go back now."

He smiles at me, like my ignorance on such things is

cute.

"I can't exactly take him to court over it, can I?" He brushes a strand of hair from my eye and tucks it behind my ear. "Promise me you'll give me no trouble. I don't want to punish you on our wedding night."

There's that word again. Punish.

"Is this how my life is to be? Punishment for disagreeing with you?"

His eyes darken. "No. Punishment is only for disobeying me. You can disagree whenever you'd like."

I stare into his eyes. They're still the icy blue from when we met, but there's a tinge of warmth I didn't see before.

Could he be softening?

I adjust my seating on his lap and feel his erection pressing against my hip. He hasn't asked for anything in return. He hasn't forced himself on me, and he was tender only moments before.

It was all a ruse to get my cooperation. There is no tenderness in him. Nothing real. This isn't a real relationship. There will be no true marriage.

This will only be me being made to bow to his dictates whenever he wants and he's not above punishment and bribery to get it.

"Either way, Kasia, by the time you fall asleep tonight in my bed, you'll be my wife," he promises in the heaviest tone I've heard him use.

In his bed.

"My father won't be there, then," I say. "At the wedding," I clarify.

"No. It will just be Margaret and my brother. I've arranged for a priest." He pinches his lips together. "I wish I could give you something more…well, more."

For a moment I thought he might say romantic. But surely nothing between us will ever be that.

This is an arrangement. I have no say in it. It's been decided. I only have to show up.

"There's time this afternoon for you to shop for a dress

if you'd like. Margaret can go with you, and two of my men." He brushes the back of his knuckles across my cheekbone. The small gestures are confusing me. I push his hand away and slip off his lap.

Tugging my dress down, I smooth out the skirt. If anyone saw what we did, what he made me do, I would be mortified. A quick look around tells me we're alone. At least from what I can see. There's always a man on guard somewhere.

"I don't—actually, yes. That would be nice." Any excuse to get out of this house. Even if it is to shop for a dress I will despise.

He looks up at me, as though he's not quite sure what to make of my compliance. Isn't this what he wanted?

My phone dances on the table and I swipe it before he can grab it. An email. Finally something that might bear fruit.

"I'll talk with Margaret. We can leave in an hour if she's able." I pick up my kindle and my untouched cup of tea. I'd come out to the yard to bury myself in a book, to forget all the mess surrounding me. But he'd only brought it out with him.

He gives a slow nod then stands from the chair. "I'll let her know. Tommy and Michael will be going with you."

I raise my chin a fraction. His cock is outlined against his trousers. I keep my gaze fixated on his chin and curl my toes into my sandals.

"Kasia." He says my name hard, and I stare at him, waiting for his next volley of instructions. "Things can be good between us, just like they were."

I laugh. The haze of pleasure has lifted. I'm no longer in the pliable mood he put me in with his titillating touch.

"Right. We'll be best of friends, Dominik." I pat his arm and leave him beneath the shade of the great weeping willow.

CHAPTER TWELVE

Dominik

"I'm so sorry, Mr. Staszek." Margaret rushes toward me as I enter the chapel. Margaret brought Kasia an hour earlier, while I finished a meeting.

"For what, Margaret?" I ask, noting the panic in her eyes. The doors to the small chapel I've arranged to use for the ceremony are closed. I couldn't give Kasia a proper wedding, but I could at least bring her to a church to say our vows before God's watchful eyes.

"I tried to convince her otherwise, but she wouldn't listen. She just wouldn't." Margaret's mouth thins.

"Whatever it is, I'm sure it's fine," I assure her. She's spent extra attention on her makeup and her dress for the night. Margaret's worked for my family for over twenty-five years, I won't have her feeling like she's to blame for something Kasia has done.

"Is she here?" I ask, suddenly aware that she could have defied me. I never gave my men permission to physically drag her here if she wouldn't comply on her own.

"Oh, yes, she's here. In that little room Father Peter was so nice to let her use."

"Okay, then whatever else it is, it's fine." I check my watch. "I think we should get started. Why don't you go get her?"

"Dominik!" Jakub comes out of the church with a wide grin on his face. "Let's get this started, huh? I have a few women waiting for me at the club." He waves me over.

I touch Margaret's shoulder. "Go on, get her ready. Let's get this over with. I'm sure she'll feel better once it's done."

Margaret frowns. She doesn't like this. A man should love his wife, she had told me after she heard my father talking about this arrangement. Diana had been my intended bride at the time. I don't think she likes how easily I've switched sisters.

"It will be fine, please." I motion toward the room she pointed out. "Go get her."

She pinches her lips together and gives me a nod. She won't give me trouble. At least not like Kasia will, I'm sure.

At least she's here. I wasn't lying when I said I didn't want to start out our marriage with a punishment. It doesn't mean she's not getting her ass smacked a few times tonight though.

"Let's go." I tug on Jakub's shoulder and head into the chapel. Father Peter is already standing at the front of the small church. They reserve this chapel for small ceremonies when the main church is otherwise used. Using the main church would have let Kasia see how empty the room was; this way, it's not so apparent.

"Too bad our father can't be here," Jakub says as we walk down the short aisle to the front of the chapel. "First born son gets married—it should be a big event."

"Waiting would be too dangerous. Garska is up to something and the sooner I get my ring on his daughter the better."

"You really think he's going to try for our territory? The council already granted it to our family."

We reach the front pew and I turn to him. I don't want the priest overhearing us. "Exactly. So, the sooner I join our families together the better. He won't have any excuses not to keep with the original agreement. And when I find what I need to prove he's behind all this legal bullshit, they'll grant me his territories as repayment."

I check my watch then look up at the priest. "Are you ready, father?" I ask.

He clears his throat and nods quickly. "Yes, Mr. Staszek. Whenever you are ready to begin."

I step forward to my spot and Jakub falls in line behind me. Three of my men stand at the back of the chapel; they act as witnesses and protection at the same time. Lena will be pissed she missed this, but our father insisted she return to Poland with him while I sorted out the mess here.

"Would you like music?" Father Peter leans toward me to ask.

I could care less, but it's tradition. Once I see Margaret in the doorway at the back of the church, I give the okay. The deep sounds of an organ play, echoing in the small building.

Margaret takes a quick glance to the side, then walks down the aisle toward me, carrying a small bouquet of white roses. She gives me a wobbly smile and moves to the pew on my side of the church. The doorway remains empty, however.

My jaw tenses, and just as I'm about to signal for my men to find her, she appears.

She's wearing black to our wedding.

"Oh, shit," Jakub laughs behind me.

Father Peter clears his throat again. The old man is uncomfortable around me to begin with, and now he sees my bride coming toward me carrying a single red rose looking as though she's headed to a funeral instead of her wedding.

Margaret's gripping her flowers so tightly, one of the stems breaks off and falls to the floor at her feet. I don't blame her for this. Kasia has her own mind and makes her own decisions.

The dress is a simple wrap that hugs her hips. A long slit in the side exposes her thigh as she walks. I'm surprised she's not wearing heels but a pair of black flats. She's left her hair down in thick waves around her shoulders, with the right side pulled up behind her ear and held back with a pearl encrusted clip. The same pearl drop earrings she always wears dangle from her earlobes.

Other than the inappropriate color, the woman looks edible. The neckline is cut deeper than I'm sure the Father is happy about, but it looks good on her. A heavier chested woman would look tacky, would probably fall out of the dress. But Kasia's subtle breasts, that fit perfectly in my palm, make the dress more elegant.

She doesn't lift her gaze from the priest as she makes her way down the aisle. It's only when she's at my side that she gifts me with a quick glance. I take her hand in mine and we face the priest.

Father Peter clears his throat again. Maybe I should have made him have a drink before we started. I'm no threat, but he's gotten it in his head we're bad people. We don't bring our business out this far into the suburbs. We stay in the city, making our money there. This is our home, and we don't shit where we sleep.

But rumors spread fast and furious. It seems the church is not immune to judgmental thoughts.

Father Peter begins his speech, but a curt shake of my head makes him skip ahead. He turns the page of his little book and goes straight to the vows.

Kasia tries to tug free of my hand when he utters the word obey, but I don't give an inch. She'll stay at my side, holding my hand, because that's where she belongs. Tethered to me for eternity.

"Kasia," I say quietly when she hesitates to repeat the words. "It's your turn." I squeeze her hand.

She swallows and abruptly turns to me. With wide eyes and flushed cheeks, she repeats every word, except one. The important one. The one I'm not going to let her get away with not repeating.

Father Peter quickly starts to give me my vows, but I hold up a hand to still him.

"Kasia, you forgot one." I narrow my eyes slightly. "We'll wait until you finish."

Father Peter looks at her with horror in his eyes. Does he think so poorly of me he thinks I'll strike her down in the damn chapel?

"I said everything I want to say," she raises her chin in absolute defiance. Poor girl thinks she's safer here, that I won't force her.

"Father Peter, if you would remind her of which vow she missed so she can repeat it." I keep my eyes locked on hers. There's a battle of wills here, and she didn't bring the right ammunition.

"Certainly," he says and goes over the vows once more. "You missed obey, my dear. If you'll just repeat them, we can move forward." There's desperation in his voice.

She's silent for a long stretch. The only sound in the chapel is the creak of the pew when Margaret moves her legs.

"Please," Father Peter says quietly. "Kasia, do you promise to cherish, honor, and *obey* your husband until death parts you?"

"I do." She squeezes my hand and averts her eyes. I could be a complete dick and make her say the words. I'm comforted by the fact that she'll be repeating an entirely different set of vows once I have her naked in my bed tonight.

Father Peter speeds through the rest of the ceremony like he's just been injected with speed. Every time she tries to tug out of my grip, I hold her tighter. Finally, it's over and he's announced us husband and wife.

He glances at her with a pitiful smile before looking to me. "You may kiss your bride," he says.

I step closer to her, capture her chin in my hand and push her head back until my mouth hovers over hers. The warmth of her breath hits me.

"Till death do us part, wife," I whisper to her, then seal our vows with a hard kiss.

CHAPTER THIRTEEN

Kasia

Dominik is silent on the drive back to his house. Margaret took the second car with two of Dominik's soldiers, leaving me alone with him and our driver. His brother left after the ceremony, giving me his congratulations and a feigned welcome to the family.

We make it through the gates of his estate within twenty minutes after leaving the chapel. The ceremony had been so short, the attendance barely notable. Not exactly what little girls imagine for their wedding days, but this isn't a real marriage. This is a sham.

I look out my window and drag in a shaky breath. I can't think this way. It brings a tightness to my chest when I consider how loveless, how empty my life is going to be. How it's been.

Lost in my own pity party, I don't feel the car park.

"Kasia, we're home," Dominik says, reaching his hand back into the car for me. I stare at it, the thickness of his fingers, the large palm. This is a man who can hurt me. He's capable of such horror. And now he's my own personal nightmare.

I place my hand in his and scoot out of the back of the black SUV. He doesn't let go when I'm on my own feet. Instead, he holds me tightly and we make our way up the stairs to the house.

Margaret's already inside. The kitchen light is on and I hear pots being moved around.

"Dominik." I pull him to a stop once we're inside. "I'm not hungry. Can you tell Margaret not to bother with dinner?" It's late, already after eight o'clock. I'd rather just take a hot shower and sink into bed. Pretend this evening didn't happen.

He stares at me with narrowed eyes for a brief moment, then gives me a small nod. "I'll speak to her. You go upstairs. I'll be right behind you."

Feeling somewhat emboldened by his granting my first request, I move forward with another.

"About that," I drop his hand. "I...we don't need to do...anything."

His lips kick up in a playful grin. I'm glad my discomfort is so amusing to him.

"But we do, Kasia." He steps closer, taking away the space I created between us. He runs his hand up my arm, snakes it behind my neck and fists my hair. I gasp, unable to get away from him. He's pulling my hair at the roots.

"Dominik."

"You remember this afternoon? When you felt so good in my lap? Don't you want more of that?" he asks, brushing his lips along my jaw. A warm shiver runs over my skin.

"I remember how you used my body against me. I remember how you played me for an idiot just to get me to agree to something, to make me pliable." I'm angry at myself for falling for it. A man like him...it's expected behavior. I should have been smarter.

He pulls back a little, lining up his blue eyes with mine. "Is that what has you so upset? Is that why you wore funeral colors to our wedding?" He twists his hand in my hair, but the pain works against me.

I don't answer him. Anything I say will be twisted against me.

Tiny wrinkles form around his eyes as he smiles down at me. "That's exactly it." He licks my lips. "If mind-bending orgasms piss you off, let's see how angry I can make you." He lets go of my hair and steps back, gesturing toward the steps. "Go upstairs, Kasia."

I want to pummel my fists into his chest. Kick my feet into his shins, but it would do no good. The man's a giant in comparison to me. The only damage that would be done would be to me.

"Kasia," he snaps my name and my eyes jump to his eyes. "Go on," he softens his tone.

I glance down the hall where Margaret is working in the kitchen. There is no hope for me. I said the words, and now I have to live up to them.

As I pass him, he touches my arm. It's a light flitter of a connection. He doesn't grab me or make any more demands, just touches me as I pass.

I climb the stairs, wondering how many nights in my life I'll be sent to his bed with such a heavy heart.

• • • • • • •

The bedroom door clicks as it closes behind Dominik. I stare out his bedroom window at the rose garden below. The solar powered lights that are spiked into the ground throughout are lit and I can make out the lush bushes with their deep red blooms.

I'm startled when Dominik puts his hands on my shoulder. For such a large man, he can move without making a sound.

"You like the gardens," he says, like he's just figured that out. Maybe he has. The past week hasn't exactly been used to get to know each other. We've avoided each other or been at odds with one another. I still know next to nothing about him.

"My grandmother had a large rose garden in her yard. It was the only flower she grew. They remind me of her," I say quietly. My father's mother had braved the risks of starting over with a new life in America. I admired her strength. "She was a strong woman," I say absently.

He squeezes my shoulder. "You're stronger than you think."

"It doesn't really matter now, does it?" I turn around in his arms and stare up at him. I've already changed out of the dress and thrown it in the garbage. I never want to see the damn thing again.

"A weak woman is no fun, Kasia. I don't like doormats."

I roll my eyes. Isn't that what he's made me? I have no choices, no options but to lie still and take what he gives me.

"Were these your grandmother's too?" he asks, touching the pearl drop earrings.

"No. My mom's. She lent them to me the day before—" I stop, not wanting to revisit one traumatic moment before living through another.

"Do you have nothing else of hers?" he asks and he sounds genuine in his curiosity.

"No." There's no need to hide things from him. Well, aside from the one thing I will never tell him — or my father until I've found out everything I need.

"Your father never gave anything to you because he blames you. If he knew these were hers, he'd take them, too," he says, and I can hear the contempt he carries for my dad.

"He would," I confirm. The ironic thing, the tragic thing about these earrings, is he gave them to my mother as a birthday present. He doesn't remember. But I do. She loved them.

He runs the back of his knuckles across my cheek. "Let's not talk about your parents right now."

"Probably a good idea," I fight back a smile.

Dominik touches his fingers to the thin strap of my nightgown. "Even though the color was all wrong, the dress you wore tonight was beautiful on you." He gently tugs the straps over my shoulders. Goosebumps pepper my flesh as his featherlike touch trails down my arms, bringing my nightgown with it.

His touch isn't new. My arousal to him isn't new, but this burning sensation inside me shakes me still. What happened last night, what took place this afternoon hasn't prepared me for this moment.

He nudges my chin up and for a brief moment I find comfort in his stare. There's a hunger lurking there, a need that matches mine.

"So beautiful," he whispers and brushes his full lips across mine. It's a tease. I reach for him when he sweeps across a second time and he presses himself against me. One hand cradles my head while the other pushes the white nightgown down until it's a pool of satin at my feet.

I bring my hands up, pressing them against his chest. I can feel him, all of him. His cock is hard against my body. The black slacks of his suit do nothing to hide it from me. He steps back a little, enough to sweep his gaze over my naked form.

He's seen my pussy before, he touched my breasts this afternoon, but this is the first time he's seen me completely nude. His gaze unsettles me, and I lift my arms to cover myself.

"No, Kasia." He brushes my arms away. "Never cover yourself. Stand there for me," he says and tugs at the tie around his neck. I'm helpless to move while he slowly tugs the black tie from his shirt.

He stalks around me, tossing his jacket to the armchair near the dresser. My skin heats beneath his attention. Fabric shuffles from behind me and when he makes his way back in my line of sight, his dress shirt is missing. Easily, he kicks out of his shoes and yanks off his socks, tossing them aside. Now he's standing in front of me, standing only in his black slacks and a white t-shirt.

I try to avert my gaze, but I can't stop looking at him. At

the strength displayed in his muscles. The dark inked tattoos on his chest peeking out of his t-shirt. Something written in Polish curves around his left bicep.

He pulls his t-shirt over his head and drops it in the same puddle as my nightgown. The black tie dangles over one shoulder.

I lick my lips. How long must I stand like this, being observed, calculated. A sense of unease creeps over me and I bend my arm, wanting to cover just a bit of myself from him. To shield myself from his prowess.

His lips spread into an approving grin. I've played right into his hands. Slowly, he pulls the tie from his shoulder, his eyes never leaving mine. With each step he takes toward me, I retreat until I'm backed against the bed.

"Let me help you, Kasia." He gently grabs my wrists and pulls them in front of me. Winding the soft fabric around my wrists, he binds them together, while leaving enough for a leash of sorts.

"Dominik," I say, but I have no idea what should come next.

He brushes my hair over my shoulders and pulls me against him. And there he is again, all strength and power.

As though he can sense my indecision, he wraps his hand around the back of my neck and pulls me into his kiss. There's nothing gentle here, just raw ownership. When he pulls back, there's a satisfaction in his eyes. He's conquering me with his touch.

"Don't stiffen up on me yet, Kasia." He cups my breast, flicking my nipple with his thumb. My nerves vibrate with his touch. Too easily I fall into him when he touches me like this.

He releases my breast and trails his hand down my torso, until he's cupping my sex. I swallow back the moan that threatens to escape.

"My wife is wet for me," he whispers into my ear. He's trimmed his beard, but it still tickles my face as he rubs his chin over my cheek. "I can practically smell your arousal."

I turn away from him. My face is too hot, I must be blushing from head to toe.

He chuckles.

One finger slides through my wet pussy lips and thrusts up into my passage. I lean into him.

"So ready for me." He kisses my cheek. "On the bed," he says and slowly pulls his finger from me.

With my hands tied, I can only sit on the mattress and scoot back onto the bed. Probably not the sexiest thing he's ever seen, but he lets it go without comment. My gaze flies to his hands that are working his belt open and then undoing the button on his trousers. He shoves his pants, along with his boxers, down and my throat clenches.

While keeping his eyes laser focused on me, he wraps one hand around his long, thick shaft.

"Lay back, Kasia," he says, climbing onto the bed, one knee between my legs. He helps me to my back then pulls the small lead of the tie up until my arms are stretched over my head. I watch his expression, the way he licks his lips, the way his jaw tightens as he winds the lead around one of the poles of his headboard.

I think he's made the headboard specially for this purpose, because in no time I'm tied to his bed.

He kneels between my open legs and looks down at me. I have no recourse now, I'm completely at his mercy.

"Remind me of your vows, Kasia," he says, covering my body with his own. The tip of his cock rests just at my entrance. He leans to the side, capturing my clit between two of his fingers.

"What?" I blink. This new pleasure he's giving me makes me lose track of the conversation.

"Your vows, Kasia. Say them for me again." He lines up his gaze with mine. "All of them."

I know what he wants. He wants my promise to obey him. I managed to get away without saying the exact wording at the chapel. The priest had taken pity on me, or he simply didn't want to see how angry Dominik could get.

"I…"

"I want to hear you say the words, go on, Kasia. Let me make you feel good, but first, you have to give me the words." He pinches my clit, sending an electric fire through to my core. Fuck, it hurts in the best way.

He's not going to let me up until I do this. He'll keep me on the brink; he'll find new ways to punish me until I give over.

There's no one else here. I can give him this. It's just us.

"I'll obey you, Dominik," I whisper. A surge of arousal sweeps through me with my vow. How many hidden buttons are there in my libido?

He grins, then kisses me. A soft kiss that leads quickly into the fierceness I've come to depend on from him. There's a gentleness to him, beneath the power, but it doesn't override the animal in him that draws out the animal in myself.

With a shift of his weight, he moves his hand and his cock is pressed against my entrance again. He slides the head of his dick through my folds, there's enough wetness to coat him.

As he slides forward, I tense, squeezing my eyes closed.

"Relax, Kasia. Don't make it harder…fuck…don't…" His lips clench together. "You have to relax. You're so tight. I don't want to hurt you."

He pushes forward more, and I hiss at the stretch. I'm going to rip. He's so much bigger than any toy I've ever used to take the edge off.

"Shhh." He cups the side of my face and forces my gaze to lock with his. "Just look at me, Kasia. Look at me, and you'll be fine," he promises, but when he moves again the pain is back.

"Please," I whine, but it's not for him to stop. No, I want more. I want it all and I want it now. My clit throbs with desire to be touched.

He swoops down and kisses me, biting down on my lower lip while he thrusts in one quick movement all the way into me. I cry out into his mouth from the instant fullness, the burning.

"Give it a second," he says, but I don't listen. I plant my feet on the bed and arch my back until I can move my hips against him.

"Fuck. You're too tight, Kasia." He holds my hips down with one hand and reaches between us with the other. "I want you to come so hard you scream down the house." He moves within me now, slowly at first, but then he thrusts harder and faster.

"Dominik!" I pull on the restraints. I want to touch him, to hold him, to dig my nails into his flesh.

He must sense my need, because he quickly unties me from the bed, and pulls the tie from my wrists. All the while he's plowing into me again and again. I grab hold of his shoulders and move along with him.

"Don't," he tries to hold my hips down, but I'm too fevered. The pain has dulled, and I want more of it, more of him.

"Hard, Kasia. Come hard." His voice is strained, raw with his order.

"Dominik!" I scream his name as I'm blindsided by the tsunami of pleasure that crashes over my body. Too fast, too hard. I scream his name again and again as the waves rip through my body.

Only as I come back down, when my breath is labored and my heart is nearly outside my chest, does he successfully pin me down and fuck me harder than I thought possible this first time. Nothing I thought I knew about this was right. I expected gentleness. Tenderness. I expected candles and flowers.

"Fuck!" he bellows and plows into me one more time and stills. His cock throbs inside me as he comes, hot sticky cum pours into my passage.

His breath is shallow when he opens his eyes and looks down at me. For a moment I think he doesn't register who I am, but quickly the confusion passes and his jaw clenches.

Easing out of me, he sits on the edge of the bed. The lighting is low, but I can make out the trail of blood on his cock. I bled.

I'm too old for that aren't I? How could that be?

Without a sound, he shoves off the bed and disappears into the bathroom. I ease my legs closed and quickly snatch up my nightgown, throwing it over my head before he comes back. The dull ache between my thighs increases with my movements. When he returns, he's wearing a pair of boxers and carrying a towel.

I let him gently push me back onto the bed and wipes between my legs. Another streak of blood dots the cloth. It's not much, but it's there.

He frowns.

"We should have gone slower," he says and brings the towel, along with his dirty suit from the floor to the closet.

Do I sleep here now, or should I go back to my room? He answers for me by pulling back the covers and gesturing for me to get under them. I press myself to the end of the bed, but once he's climbed in, he grabs me and drags me across the bed into him.

I swallow, unsure of what to say, what to think, how to feel. I'm not angry. I'm not filled with the hate I thought I'd have for him.

"Are you all right?" he asks quietly through the darkness.

"I'm fine. Are you?" I ask.

He chuckles and kisses the back of my head. "Go to sleep, Kasia."

And unlike what I promised myself I would never do, I obey my husband.

CHAPTER FOURTEEN

Dominik

Last night won't stop replaying in my mind. There're complications between us, but then last night was easy. Kasia responds so quickly, so naturally to my touch, it's hard not to get lost in her.

If I didn't have to be in the city all day, I would have rolled her over this morning and taken her again. But I have things to do, information to gather.

That's why I'm at the Katfish Klub, our newest investment, in the middle of the day. Jakub gets information better than anyone I know.

"This one?" Jakub waves over a woman from the wall. She hurries toward us in high heels, black stockings, and a shimmering dress.

"Jakub, how is she supposed to carry drinks in that get up?" I ask, waving my hand in her direction. She looks somewhat relieved that one of us is thinking. "Can you even breathe in that?" I ask her.

She looks to Jakub, who gives her a small nod. Permission to speak.

"Not easily, sir. It's a little restrictive," she says, running her hands over the leather corset.

"Fine. We'll try again." Jakub waves her away and plops down at the bar in the stool beside me. "I hate this place. Why did we buy it?"

"Because once you do what you do best, it will make us three times what the last owner was making." I remind him. "And it gives us a legitimate business."

He frowns. "Fine. I'll keep working on it." He swivels around in the stool and looks at me. "I suppose you want the information you asked me for."

"I'm that transparent, am I?"

He deadpans. "To me, you are. I mean, I'd like to think as my older brother, you come into the city for more reasons than just work, but I know you. All you do is work." He reaches over the bar and pulls out a thick manila folder. "I brought this down when I saw you pull up." He lays his hand on top of it.

"What is it?" I sigh. My brother has a flair for the dramatic. I usually play into it because he knows things I don't about people. He listens to the gossip, knows who is doing what. I don't have to do those things because he does them for me.

"Kasia has been working with a private detective for the last year." He is also a man who can get straight to the point when needed.

"What?" I reach for the folder, but he swipes it away.

"She's been paying him a monthly fee, but the guy's a washed-up asshole. He takes her money but doesn't do shit."

"What does she want him to do?" I ask. Private detectives have contacts in the police department. Having men like him poking around families like mine and Kasia's father isn't safe. She should know better.

"She wants him to find who was involved in the car accident. Apparently, she doesn't believe it was just some drunk." He finally slides the folder over to me. "What's in here is his contact information, some of the snapshots I got of him, and a few police reports. He has a rap sheet almost as long as mine." He smirks.

I flip through the folder. "What did you find in her emails?" After finding her in my office and seeing that bogus email account on the screen, I asked Jakub to find the real one. I knew she was hiding something, and I was right.

"Mostly just emails to this DeGrazio asshole. She used it for school, so there was a bunch of stuff to and from her professors."

"And her texts?" I push. She's not going to like that I've dug so hard into her life, but the means justify it.

"More of the same. A few messages to the detective wondering if he had anything — after he doesn't answer her emails. A few to a study group. She could have deleted anything important, but I doubt it."

"Why?" I ask, curious of his opinion.

He shrugs. "She doesn't exactly live the most exciting life. Her calendar was filled with school shit, tests, paper dates, graduation stuff. Contact list was short; other than Marcin she had maybe half a dozen personal contacts. Everything else was professional shit."

"Marcin kept her sheltered," I say, but there's more to it than that. People are just like things, easily taken away. If she'd surrounded herself with a lot of friends Marcin could use them against her. He could block her from them if she didn't play his games right.

"How are things with her anyway? I mean, you tie the knot last night but you're here doing business today?"

"She'll settle in. It will be fine." I check the time.

"Have you talked with Dad recently?" he asks, lowering his voice even though we're the only ones in the room. The girls have all gone off to put on the next uniform option.

"A few days ago. I talked with his attorney this morning, that's where I just came from. He's confident he'll have it all squared away by the end of the month."

"Next time you go to the lawyer, I want to go with." He raises his chin. "I should know what's going on, too."

There's a hint of defensiveness in his tone, but I don't argue with him. He's the second son and has spent more time partying than getting down to business. But I can't deny he's starting to come around.

"Of course. I'll let you know. The whole case is bullshit. They have no tangible evidence. They audited the books and came up with nothing. Not a single receipt was out of balance." That's why we pay the number crunchers so fucking well. "It's all just a campaign to cause trouble. Marcin's behind it, I know it. He stands to get everything if our family is hit hard. They'll give him our territories and none of his businesses will roll to us when he dies." Which is going to be a lot sooner than the fucker thinks, if I can prove he's behind the witch hunt that sent my father into hiding.

"And this shit with Marcin?" he prods.

"I have almost enough condemning information. Once everything's cleared here, we can take it to the old men back home." It's not much, an overheard conversation. I need the money trail, and as soon as I get that it will be locked.

"You look ready to bolt; you need to be somewhere?" He pushes my shoulder. "I have two more uniforms to show you."

"You'll have to pick it yourself. I have just enough time to make a stop before I need to be at the accountant's office on the south side. He might have the money trail we need to get permission to move forward. Just send me a picture of the one you like." I slap his shoulder and grab the folder from the bar top. "Thanks for this, Jakub."

"Yeah." He waves me off." Go. I'll just sit here and put this damn club together."

I laugh. He grumbles, but building up clubs is his specialty. He flips night clubs the way real estate moguls do houses. But this time, he's not flipping it, this time we're keeping it. Legit businesses are needed in our world, and this one will serve us well.

Erik DeGrazio, private detective, wasn't hard to find. When he wasn't at his office, his secretary pointed toward the dive bar across the street. That's where I found him. Slumped over a half drunken beer, watching the Cubs getting their asses handed to them on the big screen television. His gray shaggy hair hangs over his ears, and his thick plastic-rimmed glasses slide down his nose. He pushes them back up with his pudgy finger.

"So, this is what my wife is paying you good fucking money for," I say, sliding into the stool beside him at the empty bar. The bartender looks up at me but quickly makes the right decision and heads to the other side of the room. There're a few stragglers watching the game. But they're either too drunk or too jaded to care what Mr. DeGrazio and I are talking about.

"Who's your wife?" His words slur.

I shake my head. Washed up ex-cop probably.

"Kasia Garska. She's a Staszek now, though."

His eyes widen, fixate on me, then he looks at the door.

"You're not going anywhere," I assure him and pat his shoulder. "I just want to know what you've found out so far."

"Who are you?" he asks. Fear makes his lip tremble, or maybe it's the liquor.

"Dominik Staszek, her husband."

His lips puff outward when he blows out a breath.

"Fuck."

"Well, that depends. What information do you have for me?" I ask, pushing his beer away from him.

"Look. I haven't told her anything. I keep telling her there's nothing. I keep telling her, but she keeps sending me money and telling me to keep looking." He puts up both his hands.

"I'm not asking what you told her. I'm asking what you found." I lean closer to him. "And I don't have a lot of time, so don't fuck with me."

He nods quick and blinks several times. Maybe he's trying to reset his brain.

"Okay, okay." He blows out another breath. "The guy driving the car — according to the police report — was high as a fucking kite."

"And?" I roll my hand in the air when he pauses.

"His brakes were cut."

My interest piques.

"Go on."

"The guy, he was a small-time dealer for the Kominskis. Once I found that out, I stopped looking. I didn't tell her anything. I just let it go. But she won't."

"You keep cashing her checks though?" I'd also like to know where her money comes from, but I'll find that out later. When I question my secretive wife.

"I won't anymore," he vows with wide open eyes. I can't fault the man too much. It was smart to stop looking. Turning over rocks in my world can find a man bitten by something much worse than an angry mosquito. The Kominskis aren't a family to mess around with. Sticking his nose into that hornets' nest wouldn't have ended well for him.

"No. You won't. If she contacts you again, you call me." I pull out a business card and shove it into the chest pocket of his Members Only jacket.

"I got it," he says with a hard nod. "You really married her?"

"Yes, Mr. DeGrazio. I did." I slap his back and head toward the door. I have more questions for him, but I need him sober. I'll call on him again when he's clear headed.

But first, I have an interrogation to get to.

CHAPTER FIFTEEN

Kasia

"You have a phone call, dear." Margaret brings me the handheld while I sit beneath the willow with my kindle. It's quickly become my favorite spot. Dominik had a new set of cushioned reclining lawn chairs with a table delivered and set up beneath the tree for me.

"Is it Dominik?" I ask as I take the receiver from her. I haven't seen my husband since last night. When I woke this morning, it was to a chilled spot beside me in his bed.

"No, it's Tammy," Margaret says with confidence, like she knows her. Why would Tammy be calling on the house phone, how would she have even gotten the number? We haven't spoken since we roomed together sophomore year.

"Oh." I try not to sound surprised, but it's not like Tammy and I were close friends.

I wait until Margaret's back in the house before I put the phone to my ear.

"Tammy?"

"Hey, Kasia. One sec." The phone shuffles.

"Kasia."

My heart drops.

"Dad?"

"Your father. yes. You remember me, don't you?" There's a sharp bite to his tone. "I have to resort to tricking that housekeeper in order to get you on the phone? My own daughter? What has that asshole done?" There's no concern, only irritation.

"I'm fine. He said you were going out of town." If he's with Tammy, he must still be in the city.

"Change of plans," he says. "What have you found out?"

Does he know of the marriage?

"Dad, last night—"

"I heard. You married him. What have you found out?"

I'm not sure what I expected, or hoped he would say, but to brush it off as so inconsequential stings. I know who he is, I've felt his disapproval, but this stings still. No matter what, he's my father. My only true family.

"Nothing," I say quietly. Another disappointment. "He found me snooping."

There's a long silence.

"You found nothing?" His voice is like a boulder dropping from the mountain tops.

Doesn't he want to know what Dominik did when he caught me?

"No, Dad. There wasn't anything in his office, nothing on his computer. He probably doesn't keep his business here at the house."

"Then you need to find out what he's doing some other way. Go with him when he goes into the city. See who he's talking to."

I dig my fingernails into my knee.

"Don't you have…employees that do that sort of thing?" I ask, desperate to get away from this subject.

"I have a daughter that's sleeping with the man!" I pull the phone slightly away from my ear when he yells. "You should be able to handle this! Be useful, Kasia."

Be useful. How many times did he bark the same demand at me while I was growing up?

I lean my head back against the cushion of the chair and look up at the leaves blowing in the summer breeze above me. It's hot today.

"Kasia."

"I heard you," I whisper. "He's not going to tell me anything." I close my eyes.

"Then make him talk. Make him tell you or show you. You're a woman, spread those legs of yours and get the information I need."

My nails go further into my skin, pinching, piercing.

"How did he get you to agree for me to take Diana's place? What does he have over you? You've done something. You're doing something that is going to get you into trouble. What is it, Dad?"

"Stay out of my business, Kasia and do what you're told!"

Before I can respond, the phone is taken out of my hand. I open my eyes to find Dominik standing over me with it pushed against his ear.

"Hello?" he says, keeping his eyes fixated on me. His jaw is tight. With one hand in his pocket, he gives the appearance of being causal, but I'm learning him. He's pissed.

"Don't call this number again, old man," he says without waiting for any response from the other side of the call. "You have my direct line; you call that if you need to talk with my wife. I'll arrange something." He doesn't wait for an answer, just clicks the call off.

He looks at me then moves to the empty chair on the other side of the table and sits down. I stare straight ahead, waiting for the punishment to be announced. I spoke to my father when I said I wouldn't.

"I didn't know it was him when Margaret gave me the phone," I say, fixing my attention on the rose garden.

"I know."

"I couldn't just hang up on him," I continue, still not looking at him.

After a long silence he says, "I know."

Relief floods me. At least he's being reasonable.

"There are things about your father you don't know, Kasia," he speaks in a low volume, but he's not angry. He's being straight with me.

"I'm sure there are a lot of things about you that I don't know, that I don't want to know." I recall the night he took me. The woman he had kidnapped in order to make someone pay a debt.

"I'm not a good man. I won't say I am, but your father...there are things that I won't do that he has no trouble doing."

I blink and look past the roses, off into the distance where the brick wall surrounds the estate. Where men walk along the wall while we're out here, protecting us from the even worse men that are on the other side of it.

"Whatever the problem you have with my father is, it's your problem. You two can fight like children all you want. Just leave me out of it." I push out of my chair and start to walk back to the house.

He snatches my hand and yanks me into his lap. My chin is captured by his massive hand and he pulls me to him for a long, deep, passionate kiss that leaves my mind swirling. When he breaks it off, he rubs the tip of his nose over my chin.

"Why can't I leave you alone?" he whispers, but I don't think I'm meant to hear it. "I'm going to ask you a question, Kasia, and you have to be honest with me. If you lie, if you bend the truth or try to hide from me, you'll be very, very sorry." Any tenderness he may have had a moment ago is gone, replaced with firm demand.

"What do you want now, Dominik?" I ask. Everyone has questions for me, everyone wants answers I don't have.

Be useful.

"Why do you think the accident wasn't an accident?" He doesn't need to be more specific. I know what he's talking about, and a wave of nausea hits me. He knows.

Of course, he does.

"You don't want to stuff your fingers in me first? Make me come for you again out here before I answer you?"

"No. You'll answer me first. I'm not playing games, Kasia." He grabs hold of my hand, pushing it off my leg and exposing the crescent-shaped cuts in my leg. "While you were talking to your father?" he asks, completely ignoring what I've said to him.

"I'm going inside."

"No." He holds me in his lap. "You're going to answer my questions and without all the attitude."

I blow out a breath.

"Kasia, you're my wife now. We can make this easy between us or we can make it difficult." He touches my leg again.

"How is anything between us easy?" The only part of us that actually works without hostility is when he's making my body crave him. Sex. We're good at sex.

"Let's start at the beginning." He traces the little marks again. "First, did you do this when you were talking to your father?"

I sigh. "Yes."

He drags his eyes up to mine, there's concern there. "No more, Kasia. If he gets you on the phone, you hang up on him. Promise me."

Promises and commands, it's all everyone throws at me. "Fine."

"Look what he makes you do to yourself," he says, tapping the little cuts. There's a trace of blood in one of them. It will bruise, I'm sure.

"He didn't—" I cut myself off. "What else did you want, Dominik?"

"I want you to tell me about the accident. Why do you think there's more to it?"

Can I trust him with this? Or will he tell me to drop it like my father had when I brought my thoughts to him.

His grip intensifies on my wrist. I'm not going anywhere

until I give him what he wants.

"It just didn't seem right. The car that hit them didn't even slow down."

"Okay?" He pushes, letting go of my wrist. "He was high, Kasia. That makes sense."

"It's not just that, they'd seen him following them. It was like he was tailing them, driving ahead of them to get in front and then he'd come out of an alley and be behind them again. Like he was trying to find a way to get to them. It's not right. And no one was arrested. Not even a traffic violation."

"The driver of the other car died too," he points out.

"The drivers of the other cars on the street didn't even stick around to give a statement. They just left."

He narrows his eyes. "Then how do you know they were being followed by this car?"

I lower my gaze, take a shaky breath.

"I was on the phone with Diana."

"During the accident?"

I flick away a tear from the corner of my eye. "She was complaining about the traffic and about the weird guy following them. Mom told her to just calm down, it was just traffic. That the guy was probably just lost."

He holds my hands, and for a moment I can feel the strength seeping from him into me.

"You heard everything?" His voice dips, like he's afraid I'll run if he talks too loudly.

I swallow. "I heard my sister scream and my mom yell. I heard the crunch..." I blink a few times and suck in air. "I heard my mom..."

"What did she say?" he asks, brushing my hair from my face. "Kasia, what did you hear her say?"

"She said she was sorry." I finally turn my gaze to him. "What would she be sorry for?"

"Did you tell your dad this?"

"No," I shook my head. "Not that part. He was...upset about everything. He'd told me to pick her up. It should have been me, and then it wouldn't have happened. I would have been on time; we wouldn't have been there at that time." The same guilt runs on a loop, tearing apart my insides.

"Your dad didn't want to look into it, so you went and hired this DeGrazio guy." He fills in the rest for me.

"You looked through my phone and my computer, didn't you?" I ask, straightening my spine. "Of course, you did. You know, you don't like my father, but you two aren't that different."

He raises his brows. "We can talk about that later if you want, but right now, I want an answer to something else."

He's a man on a mission and won't be derailed.

"What?" I'm tired of all the inquiries.

"How are you paying him?"

"When my grandmother died, she left a fund for me and Diana. When I was eighteen it rolled into my control and my dad couldn't touch it. I've been using that." And it's almost gone now. "You didn't tell him to stop looking, did you?"

"He doesn't need to be involved. I have men much better than that washed-up piece of shit."

I pull back from him to take in his expression. He's serious. He's not playing with me.

"You'd have your men look into this for me?"

He cups the side of my face. "You're my wife, Kasia. If it's important to you, it's important to me. But I don't want you to ever go behind my back, do you understand? Never on your own, you don't have to do that anymore."

I doubt he understands the weight of his words. How easily he can crush me with a few syllables.

"You talked to him."

"I did." He surprises me with the truth. It shouldn't. As far as I know, he's never lied to me.

"He found something but hasn't told me, is that it?" I've suspected DeGrazio wasn't giving me information he had, but all I could do was keep pushing. Seeing the truth on

Dominik's face, I realize what a pathetic fool I've been.

"I know everything he knows, and now my men will take it from here. But Kasia, you have to swear to me no more playing detective. No paying anyone else to do it, and no talking with your father until we figure this all out."

"You can't think he had anything to do with it."

He pauses a moment. "I don't know."

"So, I just sit here while you go off every day." As much as I love reading in this gorgeous yard, there's more for me out there.

"If that's what you want, then yes. Or you can start looking for a teaching job."

I blink. I couldn't have heard him right. Dad never let Mom even think of working. He'd only let me get my degree to dangle the carrot of some sense of freedom. I don't think he ever intended to let me have a life free of him. The more control he has the more he can punish me for ruining everything for him.

"How would that work? You won't even let me go shopping without two of your men trailing around me."

He nods. "That's true. But we'll figure something out."

I'm not sure who this man is sitting with me beneath the tree. Where's his steely demeanor? It's unsettling.

"Speaking of shopping. Did you get anything else besides that funeral dress for the wedding when you were out with Margaret?"

The wedding dress was petty, I can admit that.

"No, just that."

He pats my knee. "Then you'll have to wear something in your closet." He gently moves me off his lap and stands with me. He picks up my discarded kindle and takes my hand.

"You want me to wear a dress? Why?"

"We're going out."

It's the only answer he gives me.

And once again, I find myself obeying him.

CHAPTER SIXTEEN

Dominik

Techno music vibrates the walls of the club as I walk through the side doors with Kasia at my side. She kept to herself on the drive into the city. It took a lot out of her, I think, to tell me what she did. I wonder how many times she's replayed that phone call in her mind over the years. I wonder how many times she tortured herself with the last words her mother spoke.

Marcin Garska is a fucking prick. I was never disillusioned on that fact but seeing Kasia has shown me how fast his trip to hell will be.

I'd gotten home with the intent of forcing her to answer questions. I was willing to do whatever I needed to in order to get the truth from her, expecting her to fight me. But as I marched across the lawn and saw the tension in her body, saw how tightly her eyes were squeezed closed and her fingers pressing into her flesh the way they were, the only thing that mattered was getting her off that fucking call.

Marcin threw a few threats at me when I got on the phone, but they mean nothing. He cares nothing for his daughter. The more I find out, the clearer that has become.

Jakub greets me at the entrance to the main floor. He smiles at Kasia and kisses both of her cheeks. I don't like it — him touching her, but I don't say anything. He's being polite. They're family now.

"You want the VIP room upstairs?" he shouts the question in my ear.

I glance down at Kasia. She's wearing a sparkling dress that hugs her body, showing off the curve of her hips, the small swell of her breasts. My instinct is to hide her away. Not to let anyone see her. She's mine.

"Leave it open for us," I say, as a slow melody begins to play. Kasia leans forward to see around me toward the dance floor. She's left her long, blonde hair down but I see the pearl earrings dangling. A constant reminder of who she lost. I wonder if she's wearing them because she misses her mother or if she's trying to punish herself by never forgetting.

Jakub walks off to tell the staff to leave the room open for me and I tug on Kasia's hand, pulling her toward the dance floor. She hesitates, but it only takes a small tug to get her compliance. I may not have punished her for talking with her father, and for keeping her secret, but things haven't changed. If I want her with me, she'll be with me.

Once on the dance floor, I spin around to face her, putting my arms around her waist and pulling her to me. She looks uncertain but wraps her hands around my neck. It's been years since I've moved on the dance floor with a woman, but I find my feet quickly. Kasia, to my surprise, follows my lead easily as we make our way around the floor.

She turns her cheek and presses it to my chest. The music pours over us and all I can feel is her against me. There's so much more to this girl than being a pawn for her father to maneuver. For men like me to move about.

I tuck her under my chin and continue to move to the beat. She's not wearing high heels like the other women in the club. Even though she's so much shorter than me, and fits perfectly in my arms, she wears flat shoes. Such a contradiction, my wife.

We turn once more around the floor and I'm distracted by two men standing near the stairs leading up to the VIP section. I tense. I wasn't looking for a meeting tonight, but it seems business follows me everywhere.

"I have to speak to someone, Kasia." I stop our dance and slide my hands down her arms until I capture one hand in mine.

She follows my gaze to the men and frowns.

"Okay."

I kiss the top of her head. "Do you want to wait down here at the bar, or do you want to go to the office. It won't be long." A few minutes only. Enough to get the information I've been waiting for.

She looks over at the bar. "I'll wait out here. I'll get a drink. "

I walk her to the bar, settle her on the high stool and gesture for the bartender. "Anything you want, Kasia. But not too much of it, okay?" I kiss her temple and move my mouth down her to ear. "I have plans for you when we get home."

She bites down hard on her lip. "I don't know, Dominik. I might be tired. It's been a long day," she teases me, and the simpleness of it lightens my chest.

I cage her against the bar with my arms, and bite down on her earlobe. "Try to deny me, Kasia. I dare you."

It's loud in the club, but I still hear the little gasp my words have caused. My cock is already steel hard in my pants.

"I won't be long." I kiss her once more, and gesture to the bartender she's ready to give her order. Straightening up, I pull the cuffs of my shirt from under my jacket.

Jakub meets me at the edge of the dance floor, and we take the men up to the VIP room. I'll be able to keep an eye on Kasia from there. She's a grown woman, and I have men in the club watching out for her, but I don't like the darkness rolling through me at the idea of leaving her at the bar.

"What can I get you?" Jakub asks as we all sit down at the table.

"Nothing." I put my hand up and set my firm gaze on the Kominski brothers. "What do you have for me."

"I talked to my father this afternoon," the older of them, Christopher, says. "You know he's ill."

"I do." I nod. The old man is on death's door, but that's not what interests me.

"He wants to be sure you understand we had no idea the Garska girl was promised to you." He continues, adjusting his tie.

"No formal announcement was made." There hadn't been any reason to; it was a simple marriage for alliance.

"Okay, just—" He glances at Jakub then back at me. "As long as you know, we had no idea she was connected to you in any way."

"Understood." I give a firm nod. Whatever he's going to tell me is bad. He wouldn't be so damn nervous if it was nothing.

"When we heard you were asking around about it, we came right to you," James, the younger brother interjects. The Kominski family has a small territory on the south side. There's no rivalry or competition here. But to offend my father could still cause them trouble. Our community isn't large; word spreads like wildfire between families.

"I appreciate that." I glance over the railing to where Kasia sits at the bar. She's nursing a glass of wine, swirling it around the glass, seemingly lost in thought.

"So?" Jakub knocks his knuckles on the table. "What do you want to tell us."

Christopher eyes him briefly then concentrates on me. "My father's accounting is that he was ordered to take out that car," he says, switching to Polish for this part of our conversation. Christopher leans back in the chair, as though getting the words out has lifted some weight off his chest.

"Take out the Garska car?" I clarify, schooling my features.

"Yes. He was given information of when it would be at that intersection and he was to take out the car."

"So the asshole driving, he was just one of your own targets?" Jakub asks.

Christopher nods. "He was on the hook with my father, he was gone one way or another. He chose the right way to go out."

"Chose? You mean he was alive when he drove into them?"

"Yeah." Christopher's brows crease. "How else would we have gotten the accident to look so good?"

"The brakes were cut," Jakub points out.

"We needed to make sure he didn't puss out last minute," James answers. His fingers drum on his knee.

"And how did you convince this prick to do such a thing? Kill an innocent girl and her mom?" I ask, sensing the dark clouds on the horizon.

Christopher moves in his chair again, tugs on his tie. "That's it, Dominik." He leans closer. "That wasn't the job. The job was to hit the car. There was only supposed to be one driver. We were never told who the driver was."

My chest twists.

"Walk me through this. What was supposed to happen?" Jakub picks up the conversation while I'm letting this information seep into my mind.

"That morning we got a call with where the target would be. We got our guy out there and he waited until he saw it. He followed the car until he could find a spot where he could get ahead of it and make a turn, so he'd be coming at the side."

"How'd you get him to do it, he had to know he could die?" Jakub asks, but I think it's more from curiosity than anything.

"He was dead one way or another, he was saving his family," James says. I look back at my wife; she's waving down the bartender for a second drink. The colored lights from the DJ wave over the dance floor, blues and pinks run over her skin here she sits.

"Who gave the order?" I tear my attention away from Kasia.

Christopher's jaw clenches.

"Give me the name."

"We had no idea you were connected," he reminds me.

"The name," I say with more force.

"Marcin Garska."

And with that, all sound around me stops.

"He never said it was his daughter. For fuck's sake, who does that?" James quickly says, leaning toward us.

"Marcin Garska ordered the killing of his own daughter?"

"And his wife?" Jakub adds.

"There was only supposed to be one person in the car. We got our guy at the place Marcin told us at the time he said. This wasn't our fault." Christopher's hand is fisted.

"Tell your father I'm grateful for the information. He didn't have to come forward with it, I appreciate the honesty," I say to the brothers. "There will be no retribution," I assure them and they both sink back into their chairs. The Kominski family holds no power. Petty theft rings mostly. They're good for hiring out a dirty job, like Marcin did.

"We heard you married the other Garska girl, is that right?" Christopher pushes his luck.

"I did." I stand, ending the meeting. "And I need to get back to her. If I have other questions, I'm sure I'll be able to get hold of you."

"Yeah, of course. No problem, Dominik." He holds out his hand, and I shake it. There's no bad blood here.

But there will be bloodshed by the time this is through.

Marcin Garska dug his own grave, and it will soon be time to lay him in it.

CHAPTER SEVENTEEN

Kasia

Dominik's quiet on the drive home from the club, so I've left him to his thoughts. Whatever his meeting was about has left him in a dark mood.

He pulls his phone out and grumbles while he's firing off text messages.

"Has something happened?" I ask as the SUV parks in front of the house. It's late, and I'm tired. Dominik didn't keep me at the club for much longer after his meeting. His mood had soured, I think.

The driver gets out of the car once we're parked.

"Nothing new," he says, but I sense there's more. He's not telling me everything.

I don't push. It's been a good night. I don't want to ruin it with anger. There's been so much of that over the years in my life, I don't want to carry any more of it into my future. I won't delude myself with the idea that I'll have a happy, love-filled marriage, but we don't have to be enemies.

It's that idea I'm grasping onto. I just don't want to be hated anymore.

Dominik climbs out of the car and grabs my hand, tugging me out with him.

I watch him as we walk up the stairs to the house. His jaw is tense, his back is locked up. There's more tension than when we left home earlier.

Home. That's what this place is for me now. My home.

As soon as we're inside the house, the door's closed and locked, he turns on me, walking me into the front door and caging me in with his arms. I can smell the brandy on his breath, and it intoxicates me.

"We should go upstairs," he says, kissing me hard, like he's been waiting all night to do this. To get his mouth on mine. I bring my hands up to his hips, holding him to me. I've been waiting all night, too.

"It's not safe here? I thought you said your men know not to watch what's not their business?" I tease, hoping to bring some light to his dark.

"Don't worry, you're safe here." He captures my face in both hands. "You're safe with me, Kasia."

The weight of his words pins me in place.

He kisses my forehead, then grabs my hand again. "Upstairs, wife." He emphasizes the last word.

I see a flicker of a shadow in the kitchen. Margaret's still here, and I don't want to put her in a position where she sees or hears something uncomfortable, so I follow him upstairs without any further teasing.

Once we're in his bedroom, though, I untangle my hand from his and step away, flicking my hair over my shoulder.

"I'm pretty tired, Dominik." I fake a yawn. "Maybe I'll just head to bed."

His eyes nail my feet to the floor. With purposeful, slow steps he stalks toward me. A lion to his prey. My heart beats out a loud melody against my chest and my mouth dries.

When he reaches me, he grabs the small handbag from my hand and tosses it to the dresser. With both hands he grabs my shoulders and spins me around. I can see his face in the mirror, his lips are pressed into a thin line, his eyes set firmly on me.

He picks up my hair and pushes it over my shoulders, exposing my back to him. The zipper of my dress lowers, while his gaze rises to meet mine in the mirror. The little straps of the dress sag down my shoulders. With a featherlike touch, he skims his fingers over my shoulders, pushing the straps down completely. The dress, a simple, black, deep-cut dress, falls to my feet.

I stand in front of him in only my black strapless bra and panties. He licks his lips.

With a flick of his fingers on my bra, the clips are unfastened, and it falls away from my body. I move to catch it, to hold it to me, but he grabs my arms, pinning them to my side.

"Are you trying to deny me, Kasia?" His voice is heavy, raw.

I catch his gaze in the mirror again and a shiver runs along my spine. His fierce expression should spread terror through me, instead of making my panties so damn wet for him.

"If I am?" I can't help but tease him again. This is a game we're playing, and no matter who loses, we'll both win.

His lips crack into a wide grin and he steps closer to me, until his hard cock is pressed against my ass cheeks. "What do you think will happen?" he asks, wrapping an arm around me and cupping my breast. "Do you think you're allowed to deny me?" Two fingers close around my nipple and pinch, bringing with it a glorious burn.

I shake my head.

"No?" He twists my nipple and pulls forward. The intensity makes me gasp, but I don't try to pull away.

"No," I finally manage to say.

He lets go and kisses the side of my cheek. "Good girl. Let's try another question." His hand roams to my other breast. "What happens when you're a bad girl, Kasia?"

His fingers close tight, he pulls right away giving me no chance to grow accustomed to the sensation. I lean forward a bit, trying to lessen the pressure, but he's pressed to me so hard, I have nowhere to go.

"What happens to bad girls, Kasia?" he asks again, scraping his teeth along my shoulder.

"You punish them," I say while sucking in a breath.

"How do I punish you?" He gets more specific, lessening his grip.

I drag my gaze back to the mirror and find him staring at me. That same dangerous look in his eyes.

"You deny me pleasure." I answer him firmly. I won't lose this game. If he's looking for a reason to punish me, he won't find one. I'll take what he dishes out, but I will not be denied.

"No, Kasia. I deny you release. I'll give you all the pleasure you want." He spreads his fingers out on my stomach, pushing me against him more. "But you were a good girl tonight, Kasia." He moves from my stomach, reaching into the pocket of his pants.

I tense at the sight of a pocketknife in his hands.

"Don't worry," he kisses my cheek. "You're safe here, remember. You're safe with me." He kisses me again, a tender gesture as he slides the blade between my hip and the thin strap of my panties. With one arm now draped over my chest, pinning me to him, he swipes the knife, easily cutting the strap then moving to my other hip. Again, he cuts the fabric then tosses the knife onto the dresser.

"Such a pretty girl," he whispers into my ear, pulling the remnants of my panties from between my legs and dropping them to the ground.

The darkness in him reaches his eyes, I can sense it with his touch. He needs this, he needs to have this control, to have me bend to his will. What surprises me is how much I crave it too. I want to calm his storm, and I want to lose myself in it at the same time.

I reach over my shoulder and cup his cheek. At first, he stiffens, but then softens, leaning into my hand.

"I'm safe here." I stare at him in the mirror. The heat I

see, the hunger screaming at me in his reflection kicks my heart into a gallop. I swallow back a little gasp when he cups my breast again.

"You're stronger than you think, my Kasia." He lowers his mouth to my neck, scraping his teeth over my skin again. A shot of electricity jolts me, and I feel alive. More alive than I have in a long time.

It's not just that he says these things, it's that I believe him. It's that I know he believes them.

He grabs hold of my arm and spins me to face him. "I'm going to show you what a brave girl you really are." He walks me backward until my ass hits the dresser. "Down, my Kasia. Kneel for me." He presses lightly on my shoulders and I sink to the floor for him. Kneeling at his feet, looking up at him, wondering what he wants from me next. Because I want to give it to him. I want to make this good for him. To make him forget his stress.

He runs his thumb over my bottom lip. "Such a pretty mouth. I wonder how pretty you'll be with my cock stuffed inside it." His other hand works his belt open and he tugs his pants down until his cock is freed.

I try to move back, but I have nowhere to go. Still holding my head, he presses me against the dresser. I'm trapped.

"Open for me, Kasia." He fists his cock with one hand, bringing the tip to my lips. There's a pearl of moisture that is too tempting not to lick away.

He hisses as though I've hurt him with my tongue on his dick.

"Open." This order is rougher, his fingers tighten in my hair.

I bring my hand up, ready to wrap it around his shaft, but he brushes it away.

"No. Put your hands on your knees. I want just your mouth, Kasia. I'm going to fuck it and fuck it hard. If you do a good job, I'll stuff my cock in your pussy next. It's wet for me, isn't it? You're waiting for me to fuck you hard?"

He switches between Polish and English as he talks, but I manage to keep up well enough to understand him.

I open my mouth and steel myself for whatever he's going to do to me. This is his moment. He may hurt me, but he won't harm me.

He doesn't need to tell me that or explain it. It's just there, written in his eyes.

"Fuck." A buzzing sounds and he pulls his phone out of the pocket of his pants, throwing it onto the bed without looking at it.

There's no warning. He plows into my mouth, the tip of his cock hitting the back of my throat. I swallow, sputter, trying to catch my breath, but my husband isn't gentle. He never promised he would be.

I press my fingernails into my thighs, taking the face fucking he's dishing out. Again, he pushes down my throat and I swallow, but it doesn't help. I gag. He pulls out enough for me to get my breath, but that's it. The moment I'm better, he shoves himself down me again.

"Mouth stuffed with my cock," he mutters above me, thrusting again. "So…fuck…" his words trail off into a groan.

In the next moment, his dick is yanked from me and he hauls me to my feet. Have I done something wrong?

"Did I hurt you?" I ask when I see the darkness of his expression.

The stern set of his jaw softens, and he laughs.

"Hurt me? Woman, you're going to kill me if we keep that up." He steps back and quickly undresses, tossing his clothing to the floor. Once he's stripped and bare, I stare at him openly.

There's a scar on his abdomen, and I touch it lightly. He grabs my wrist, bringing it up to his mouth and kissing it.

"You were hurt," I say stupidly.

"I healed." There's more to his words, I think. A statement directed at me, but I don't understand it.

Keeping my wrist in his hand, he brings me to the bed

— his side. He opens the bedside drawer and brings out a pair of handcuffs.

"So you don't get in my way." He works them around one wrist, then spins me around to cuff the other behind my back. My shoulders pull at the position, but it's not enough to stop him. I doubt he'd listen anyway.

I press my ass back at him. There's no explanation for it, but I want his touch. Hard or soft, I just want it on me.

He's quick to react, throwing me over the side of the bed. Over and over again he smacks my ass with his open palm.

"What did I do?" I ask, unsure if I'm supposed to be enjoying his manhandling as much as I am.

"Nothing, my Kasia. You've earned a reward," he says, and increases the force of his spanks. He spreads them out over both cheeks and then my thighs. Quickly, my mind begins to fall into haze, a sweet hum covers my flesh.

But he's not done with me.

I clench and cry out with the sharpness of his nails digging into my tender flesh. He drags his hand up one thigh and then the other. My mind is focused again, but there's a calm in my soul that wasn't there moments ago.

"There's my girl," he says and moves behind me. "Ass up, I'm going to fuck you now." He pulls my hips upward to where he wants them. My face stays rooted into the bed, but I manage to get my feet planted.

In one savage thrust, he's inside me. His balls hit my pussy. There's no reprieve for me. He drags out only to slam back into me. My face rubs against the quilt covering the mattress.

"Fuck, you're so tight." He sounds like an animal gone mad. I've done that to him, I've brought him to such high arousal. I arch my back and lift my ass higher for him.

He uses one hand to grip my hip while the other moves to my cuffed wrists. He's riding me. My mind conjures up the image of how he looks riding me like the wild animal he is.

"Dominik!" I cry out. I need more, harder, faster, just more of everything. It's like I'm chasing down a ghost and I need Dominik to help me find it.

"Don't worry, sweet Kasia." He wraps his hand beneath me, quickly finding my clit.

"Oh fuck!" I yell and spread my thighs a bit more so he can have more access.

"Go on, Kasia. Show me how hard you can come while I'm riding you. Go on," he rubs my clit faster, presses harder while he keeps plowing his cock into me.

My shoulders burn, but the pain only melds into the throbbing of my ass, the ache inside of me.

Out of nowhere, a flash happens and screaming. SO much screaming. It takes a second for me to realize it's me. My body shakes, and I'm still crying out as the powerful waves wash me away.

Dominik chuckles behind me, rubbing my clit slower. He's easing me down from heaven, and only when I've landed softly does he go back to fucking me hard.

"So good," he says, tugging on my wrists and fucking me so hard the bed scratches the floor when it moves.

A smack to my ass, another grunt, a hard thrust and then he roars. His cock stills inside of me, but I feel every pulse of his release.

Dominik is heavy when he falls forward over my body. He releases my wrists, but his chest is pressed against my back. His hot breath washes over my cheek. I keep silent, letting him find his way back to me in his own time.

He presses a warm kiss to my cheek.

"Good girl," he says in Polish and slowly slips from my pussy. He undoes the cuffs and tosses them away. When he stands me up, he rubs my arms. They burn, but it's nothing compared to the pleasure I see in his features. He has a crocked smile on his lips.

"A towel?" I ask quietly, tearing my gaze from his. I have to be careful. We're good at this, at fucking, but it's the in-between times when I need to be cautious.

"No." He brushes my hair from my face. "We're married. My seed stays right where I put it." He pulls the quilt back from the bed and motions for me to get inside.

I climb inside the bed, tugging the quilt to cover myself once I'm on my side of the bed. He goes about the room, grabbing his discarded clothing and my dress before bringing them to the closet. I snuggle into the bedding.

My eyelids are heavy and there's a weakness to my muscles after such an intense release.

He walks to my side of the bed wearing a pair of pajama pants. They hang low on his hips, showing off his sharp cut muscles.

Dominik sits next to me, caressing my cheek.

"I have to do a few things. Go to sleep, I'll be up in a bit." And then he kisses me. Not the possessive way he has before, but with tenderness. It's not a kiss that forces me to realize he's in charge, that he owns me. No. This kiss gives me an entirely different feeling. A warmth spreads across my chest.

"Sleep," he says again and flicks off the light on my nightstand. I pull the covers up to my chin as he walks out of the room. He turns off the main light and closes the door quietly.

We don't have to be enemies, I remind myself. But I can't help but wonder if I'm betraying my family. Because it's not a matter of hating him now…I'm starting to like him.

CHAPTER EIGHTEEN

Dominik

I sit back in my office chair, staring at the ceiling. I've gone over the information five times, and it never changes. Marcin Garska wanted his daughter dead. He put a hit on his own daughter. But he killed the wrong one, and he's punished Kasia for it ever since.

My phone dances on my desk, and I grab it.

"Dominik."

"Yeah, Dad. It's me." I tap my fingertips on my desk. Kasia is upstairs asleep. I shouldn't have left her. I should have climbed into bed with her like I wanted to and wrapped myself around her. But I have to get this shit done.

"I just got out of the meeting."

I sent him the information I received from the Kominski brothers while we were driving home from the club. I didn't realize he'd act on the information so quickly.

"How'd it go?" I roll my head to the side. There's tension in my neck.

"Exactly like we hoped. Garska is going to lose his territory. I need you to go to the attorney tomorrow. He thinks he can get the case tossed out, but he needs your help." Code for cash. The attorney has finally figured out which wheel needs the oil. "As soon as I get home, we'll take care of Garska. We have full authority over the matter."

"That's good," I say, but there's still a dark cloud hanging over my head. Take care of Garska means only one thing, and after the way he's treated Kasia I should be glad. But I don't want her hurting, and as fucked up as it is, this will hurt her.

"His daughter. You still have her?"

"Kasia? Yes, she's here." Where the hell else would my wife be?

"She'll be the one to inherit once he's taken care of. I had to make that compromise. Instead of everything rolling over to us like the original agreement states, it will go to her. Seeing as you're married to her now, the council thinks it's fair enough. We'll need to figure out what to do with her."

My stomach twists. "She's my wife. There's nothing to decide. Her inheritance goes to me."

There's a beat of silence. My father is still the head of our family. I have never nor will I ever dispute that, but when it comes to Kasia, she's all my responsibility.

"You're right. We'll work out the details. As soon as the attorney gives the okay, we'll be on a plane home. And it could not be too soon. Your sister is driving me up a fucking wall here."

I laugh. "Not enjoying her time there?"

"The girl has snuck out so many times, our men are threatening to seal her bedroom door closed." He talks about her like it's annoying, but I know he's proud of how strong his daughter is. She's not one to follow the line just because it's where she's supposed to be.

"She'll settle down eventually." I doubt it will be any time soon, but she's his prize and I won't remind him that it's his own doing that she's so pigheaded. The girl needs a good taming.

"From your lips to God's ear, Dominik." He laughs. "How about your brother? I left him a voicemail, but he hasn't called me back."

"He's working his magic with the Katfish Klub. He's doing good work." I should probably call him or stop by his place soon. I've spent too much time away dealing with dad's legal shit and now Kasia.

"What a fucking name. You gonna change it?"

I grin into the receiver. "He's working on it. I'm giving him full responsibility with the club. He's good at it." It also keeps his hands as clean as I can keep them, but I don't say that to my father. I'm the oldest. I'll take the risks for all of us.

I catch a glimpse of a shadow passing my office door. A light goes on down the hall, in the kitchen.

"This is good, son. You've done good."

Pride blossoms in my chest. My father's never been one to lay on the compliments, but he's always given credit when it's due.

A cabinet opens and closes in the kitchen. With the dead quiet of night, I can hear almost everything happening in there.

"Thank you." I check the time. Three in the morning; she should be asleep. "Is there anything else you need from me?"

"Just handle the attorney and call me when it's all set. I'm eager to get home and get this mess dealt with."

I laugh. "I thought you'd be enjoying yourself over there. You're always saying you want to spend more time there."

He grunts. "I've had enough fun." What he means is he's had enough of not being in full control. Over there, he has to answer directly to the council. Here in Chicago, he has more freedom. Soon we won't have to answer to the council at all, but it takes time for such freedom.

"I'll call you when I get the all clear. I'm sure it won't be long."

"Good. Good."

A female voice beckons him on the other side of the line, and he makes an excuse to hang up. I put my phone on my desk and follow the soft beeping coming from the kitchen.

Kasia stands in front of the microwave, staring through the door at the small plate rotating inside.

"Shouldn't you be sleeping?" I ask in a low voice.

She jumps and spins around, her hand to her chest. "Shit. You scared me." She turns back to the microwave and hits the end button. Whatever she's reheating, it's only been in there for a few seconds.

"What are you doing up?" I walk around the kitchen island to her. She opens the microwave door and pokes her finger inside. Looking over her shoulder, I see what she has, and a smile tugs at my lips.

"I woke up and couldn't fall back asleep. I was hungry," she says and pulls the plate of blueberry pierogi from the microwave.

"Are those warm enough?" I ask as she shimmies past me to sit on a stool on the other side of the island.

"These are best room temperature, but Margaret put them in the fridge."

"She wasn't sure you'd have them today. I told her to put them away." I grab the sour cream from the fridge and the sugar bowl from the coffee nook.

"You asked her to make these?"

"She was making potato and cheese pierogi for tomorrow and I said you'd probably like some blueberry ones." I shrug like it's not a big deal. And it shouldn't be. A housekeeper making something for her to enjoy isn't a big deal. But the way her eyes light up tells me this is much bigger to her than I could have thought.

"Thank you," she says as she opens the sour cream. "It's best like this, right?" She smiles as she scoops a spoonful of sour cream onto her plate and then sprinkles sugar on top to mix.

"It is." I lean my forearms on the island across from her. I want to give her space; she seems so carefree at the moment. If I could capture it in a bottle, I would. She's so relaxed. So sweet looking.

"My grandmother used to make these for me when I was younger. When she lived with us." She uses the side of her fork to cut into the pierogi, and blueberry juice spills out. Sweeping it through the sugary cream, she brings it to her mouth.

As soon as her lips close around the treat, her eyes roll, and she moans. "I'd forgotten how good these are," she says. My cock doesn't understand she's talking about her dessert. I'm getting hard watching my wife eat something as simple as a blueberry pierogi.

"Your grandmother made them often?" I'm enjoying her smile too much, I think. It's the middle of the night. She's swept her hair into a messy ponytail, and she's wearing a cotton t-shirt and shorts. She couldn't look more innocent and at home. I could eat her alive right where she sits.

"They were a treat." She takes another bite.

"Treat for what?" I ask grabbing the container from the fridge. She's almost done with what she's heated up, and she's going to want more.

I want to see her eat more.

"For when Dad was in a mood."

I turn away from the microwave and look at her. "What does that mean?"

She tilts her head. "I know you already know. My father wasn't exactly my biggest fan. Sometimes he was cold. My grandmother tried to make up for it."

The microwave beeps and I take out the plate, bringing it to her. She takes the extra pierogi with a smile.

"With blueberry pierogi?" I ask with a grin as she wipes a small bead of blueberry juice from her chin.

"It would be our time. Sometimes Dad would take Diana out on a trip or something and she'd make something special just for us two."

"Because he left you at home?" There's an angry knot forming in my stomach.

She sighs. "I don't want to talk about my father anymore." She pops another bite into her mouth. "So, what did you find out about the car accident? I know you found something out, I could see it in your face when you came down from that meeting."

I raise my eyebrow. "Really. You know it's about that and not something else?" I tease. Fuck. When did I start being so damn playful?

I move around the island until I'm next to her. Picking up the last bite from her plate, I swipe it through the cream then bring it to her lips.

"It's late, Mrs. Staszek. Eat your snack." I push it into her mouth with our eyes locked in a heated exchange. She licks her lips and smiles. "Now I can have mine." Before she can anticipate my movements, I pluck her from the stool and put her on the island, sweeping her plate out of the way.

"Dominik!" She tries to sit up, but I point a steady finger at her.

"You had your dessert, now I'm having mine. Lay there and be a good girl for me."

She tucks her lower lip between her teeth and moves gently back down. Her shorts are easy to tug off, so I pull them past her feet and toss them onto the stool. I grab her ankles and pull her closer to the edge for me until her ass touches the edge.

"Open these pretty thighs for me, sweet girl." I push her knees down until her pussy is on display for me.

"Dominik. What if someone comes in?" She inches her hand down toward her pussy, but I grab hold of her wrist.

"Try to block me again, Kasia, and I'll spank this pussy until it's red. Understand?"

It's dim in the kitchen, but I can still see her cheeks blush.

"But someone might see," she says again, not heeding my warning.

I pull one leg up high and to the side then bring my hand down hard on her pussy. She jumps.

"Bad girl," I chide her and bring my hand down again and once more before I bring my gaze from her wet, wanting pussy to her face. She's biting down hard on her lip; her pupils have widened so much I can't see any more of her brown irises.

"Are you going to be a good girl, Kasia?" I ask, raising my hand again. I'll deliver another swat if I need to, but she's gotten the idea, I think. My girl loves pain, but she wants my mouth on her pussy right now. I can see it, feel it coming off her in waves.

"Yes, Sir."

"That's a very good girl." I put her leg back down and take my place between her thighs. "Keep your hands away."

I bring my mouth over her pussy, sucking in her clit before she has time to register my intent.

She draws in her breath, but I'm more concerned with feeding the beast inside of me. The one that wants to hurt and soothe her. I scrape my teeth over her clit, then suck it lightly until she whimpers.

"Your pussy is smooth. I like this," I say, kissing her just above her clit.

She's grabbing the sides of the island, better to keep her hands away, I suppose.

"Fuck, you taste good." With two fingers, I spread her pussy lips open and run my tongue up from her entrance to her clit, then take it in my mouth. The sounds the woman makes drive me to the brink. My cock is hard, but this isn't about me. This is about giving her pleasure for the point of pleasure. The woman has spent her entire life waiting her turn. She's in the front of the line tonight.

I slide two fingers into her tight passage, twisting them as I fuck her with them.

Running my tongue through her folds, I find her clit again, flicking it harder and harder before circling it and scraping my teeth over the sensitive bud. I continue to swirl around it, listening to her labored breathing, her moans of pleasure.

"Be a good girl for me and come hard. I want to hear you," I command, not taking my fingers away from her cunt for a moment. I bend my fingers, plow harder.

"Someone might hear," she complains softly.

"Let them. Let them hear me make my wife come so fucking hard the roof shakes." I want to growl, the need to hear her come unraveled is so great.

Her thighs start to tremble, I can feel her winding up tight. She's going to unleash any second. I turn my hand so my fingers are diving deeper into her passage and press downward as I fuck her with them.

"That's a good girl," I say, licking her from opening to clit. "Good girl. Such a good girl. Come for me, make it hard, be good. So, fucking good." I add a third finger and twist harder, fuck her harder with my fingers and flick my tongue harder on her clit. Around and around until I feel the tremors starting.

"I said come!" I growl then suck her clit into my mouth, flicking the very tip with my tongue while plowing my fingers into her with more force.

"Dominik! Dominik!" She screams my name over and over again while her body unravels in my hands. Her ass comes off the countertop and she bucks up against my mouth, fucking my face, riding my mouth until she finds the very end of her release.

I slow my fingers, ease off on her clit and press one more kiss to her sex before slipping from her. There's a small puddle beneath her ass on the counter. Her pussy juices and my saliva mixed together.

When I stand to my full height, she's staring up at me, her eyes wide and her cheeks red.

I pick up her pajama shorts, but she grabs my hand.

"Dominik." She says my name with hunger.

I look down at her. "Do you want something?" I say, and I hope to hell she does. I won't push her; this was for her.

"You." She reaches down between her legs and pulls on my own pants.

"You want what from me?" I ask. I'm going to make her

say it. I'm going to make her beg for it, if it's what she really wants.

"I want you to fuck me." She doesn't hesitate. Gone is any hesitation. "Fuck me hard."

I drop her pajama shorts and grab her legs, yanking her toward me. I have to move up to my toes, but it's not a problem. With one tug, my pants are down, and my cock is at her entrance. In another moment, I thrust inside her cunt.

"Fuck," I groan as her cunt wraps tightly around me. She's hot and slick and so fucking snug.

"Harder," she begs me. "Please, harder." She has her hands in her hair, tugging. My girl wants it to hurt.

I can do that.

I hold nothing back. I plow into her with everything I have. The sounds of our bodies slapping against each other fill the room. Her ankles rest on my shoulders, and I slide my hands up her shirt, pinching her nipples.

She moans with the bite. It's the sweetest fucking sound I've ever heard.

"Are you going to come again for me?" I ask, plowing into her so hard my balls bounce off her ass.

"Yes, sir," she cries out.

"First. Kasia. Tell me. Who owns you? Who owns this body? And you. Who do you belong to?"

No hesitation.

"You, sir! You, Dominik!" She doesn't take a second longer. I pinch her nipples, twist them to the right and like a firecracker she goes off again. It's those words that rip the last shred of control I have from my grip and I'm thrown into a whirlwind of pulses and flashes. I thrust once, twice, and then I still as everything inside of me explodes.

Electric shocks ride up my spine, up and down, while my cock unleashes inside her tight pussy.

"Fuck," I growl over her as the last of my release twitches my body. My muscles soften, and my breath starts to come easier. Her hand is on my chest, lightly stroking me.

As gently as I can, I ease her legs from my shoulders. My

cum leaks out between her folds when I pull out of her, adding to the mess we've already made. I tug my pants up and reach around the island for a towel hanging off the drawer.

"You're cleaning me?" she asks in a husky voice.

"I'm wiping the counter. Margaret doesn't get paid enough to clean this up." I smack her thigh. "Come on, get up." I help her from the countertop and hand her her own bottoms. She slides them up her thighs, covering her gorgeous curves.

"Think you can sleep now?"

She yawns. "I suppose so."

"Such a smart ass." I finish cleaning off the countertop and toss the dirty towel into the laundry room as we pass it.

"Better than a dumbass, I guess," she jokes.

She jogs ahead of me, laughing as she makes her way back up the stairs. The sound of her levity, the happiness I'm seeing, it warms me.

I have to be careful. Letting her get too close will make her dangerous. Will make her unsafe.

But for the moment, just this moment, I'm going to enjoy the sweet sound of my wife's laugh as she leads me up to our bed.

CHAPTER NINETEEN

Kasia

I wake up again to an empty bed, rolling over to his side of the bed and pulling his pillow to me. It smells of him, all spice and leather. This is the third time in as many days that he's left before sunrise.

I've been his wife for two weeks. My father hasn't tried to contact me in any way. It's a good thing that he stays away. It means I don't have to be the one to ignore him. I don't have to be the bad daughter.

But I can't help but wonder why he's disappeared. Maybe I finally ran out of purpose for him.

My alarm on my phone dings. Time to get out of bed and do something with myself. I've been sending out resumes and applying for teaching jobs in the area. Most of the schools have already hired for the upcoming year, so the options are limited. I'm still unsure how this will work since Dominik has a man following me everywhere I go, but I'm hopeful.

For the first time, I cradle hope like the fragile being it is. He's promised I can work. I can have some purpose besides simply being Mrs. Staszek, but I'm not sure any school district will approve of me bringing an armed guard into the classroom.

When I grab my phone, there are several email notifications. Maybe I'm getting an interview.

Sitting up in bed, I swipe open the app and thumb through the garbage until I find a long-awaited message. My stomach trembles as my thumb hovers over the icon. Finally, the private detective has something for me.

Dominik made me promise not to continue my digging into the accident, but this isn't continuing. This is simply reading a message. I don't have to act on it, and if it turns out to be something worth looking into, I'll let Dominik know.

Kasia, I found a link you might find interesting. Too dangerous to put it in writing. Can you meet me today, two o'clock usual place?

I stare at the message. I haven't heard from this guy in weeks. Dominik knows about him, so why isn't he going to Dominik? Why ask me to meet him?

I stare at the empty side of the bed. He might not be home until late. I can text him, but I know his answer. He'll tell me to leave it and he'll look into it.

This isn't about his sister. This is my responsibility.

I wait another minute before answering him. Hoping, I guess, that some sense will ease into my mind, but it doesn't. So, I promise him I'll be there.

Just as I hit the send button, there's a knock on the bedroom door that startles me.

"Kasia, are you up?" It's Margaret.

I blow out a breath. It's not like Dominik has me on video surveillance or anything.

"Yeah. One sec." I scoot out of bed and grab the robe next to the bed. It's a rare morning that I wake with my pajamas still on.

After tying my robe's belt around my middle tight, I open the door. Margaret's there with a large smile.

"Just wanted to be sure you were up. You said you wanted to be up by eight."

"I did. Thank you. I have an alarm on my phone, you don't have to worry about me, Margaret." She's kind and attentive. Much like my mother was.

"Well, I also made crepes for breakfast and I didn't want them to get too cold before you came down." She shrugged.

"You spoil me."

"You deserve to be spoiled," she says with a serious tone. "Mr. Staszek just called; he's going to be gone for the evening. He said he'd call you later this afternoon."

"I want to go out this afternoon. Are any of the guys around? I know Dominik won't like it if I go out alone." It would make things easier if they were all with him or off doing jobs. But I have no luck in this department.

"Of course. Tommy is here today. I'll let him know you have plans." She turns to go. "Don't forget, crepes!" She waves as she walks away.

Tommy will be with me all afternoon, but I can work with that.

I think.

• • • • • • •

"Are you ready to head home?" Tommy asks me as we head to the car after the fifth store I made him follow me around in. I haven't bought anything; I'm not even looking for anything. Apparently, Tommy dislikes window shopping as much as I do. But there's a purpose this afternoon, so it's not so annoying to me.

I check the time on my phone.

"Almost." I look down the street. "I'm thirsty. Let's stop in there." I point at the diner two storefronts down.

"There's a bottle of water in the car," he reminds me.

"I want something to eat, too. C'mon, Tommy. I'll buy you a BLT." I slide my arm through his and tug on him.

He looks down at me, annoyance dancing in his eyes.

"Fine. But not too long, all right? Traffic back home is gonna suck if we stay out here too much longer," he complains, but walks with me to the diner.

When we enter the diner, there's plenty of open tables, but it's the one in the far corner booth that has my attention. Erik DeGrazio is already in our booth, sucking down a beer. He looks up when the door shuts behind us, and his face drops when he sees Tommy.

Getting rid of him will be almost impossible.

"Think you need to use the washroom?" I'm terrible at this.

He looks at me like I've grown a second head. "No. I'm fine. Let's just get you something to eat." He heads toward a booth in the other corner of the restaurant at the windows.

I stand frozen staring at DeGrazio. Considering all the times I had to sneak around behind my father's back trying to get close to my sister when I was grounded from her, you'd think I'd be better at this.

"I have to go to the bathroom," I blurt out. Tommy stops at the booth and turns to look at me. Two other people also look up from their food to see what lunatic just made such an announcement.

"Okay, then go." Tommy gestures toward the back of the diner.

"Right," I say and hurry away. Thanks to my utter failure at being casual, I can feel his stare on my back as I make my way to the restrooms. As I pass Mr. DeGrazio's table, I catch his eye and jerk my head toward the restrooms. His gaze darts away from me toward Tommy, and he stays planted.

Once I get inside the two-stall restroom, I wait. Hopefully, Tommy lost interest when I was out of sight and is sitting at our booth.

The door opens and Mr. DeGrazio peeks his head in.

"What are you doing?" he asks in loud whisper.

I grab hold of his arm and tug him inside.

"That's one of Dominik Staszek's guys out there." He points to the door.

"I know." I nod. "Just be fast, and I'll get back out there

before he gets all nosey. So, what did you find?"

He frowns. "I tried calling him, but he didn't answer my call." He pulls out an envelope and shoves it at me. "Here's what you need to know, do whatever you want to do with it. I'm done. Like I told him, I'm not looking into anything else. And I won't take any more money from you. But this—" He points to the envelope. "Is worth what you've paid so far."

"Is this everything you already told Dominik?" I press before he has a chance to run off.

"There's more here than I remembered when I was talking him." He shrugs. "Helps to talk to a man when he's sober if you want all the information. But I'm done, Kasia. No more." He smacks his hands together, washing himself of me.

"I got it." I look down at the thick envelope. "Thank you." My words are said to an empty room. He's gone.

I straighten out the prongs of the envelope and open the top. Pictures, reports, and handwritten notes are haphazardly stuffed inside. I pull out the pictures, flipping through them quickly. Accident scene pictures — I've seen most of these already. I skip the ones with my sister and mother still inside. The police reports don't have much information in them that I don't already have memorized.

His notes though, these are what I want. I quickly read over the scribbles. His handwriting changes several times. I can tell exactly when he'd been drinking and when he'd been sober.

"Kasia!" Tommy knocks on the door. "Kasia, are you okay?"

"Just washing my hands!" I yell back and keep sweeping my eyes over the notes.

By the time I'm done reading, I'm grateful for the toilet being so close. I run inside an empty stall and vomit. Even the bitter taste left behind once my stomach is completely emptied is better than the sickness inside my soul.

The door to the room bursts open.

"Kasia." Tommy's behind me. "Kasia," he lowers his voice as I sink to the floor of the bathroom, the damning papers clutched to my chest. He squats next to me. "We're going home."

I tighten my hold on the papers when he tries to take them away from me and he gives up.

"Can you walk or am I carrying you?" he asks, and I can tell he'd rather not touch me. Carrying the boss's wife might not give him any positive points with Dominik.

My mind blanks, and I switch to autopilot. Standing up, I turn sideways and move around him out of the stall. The toilet flushes as I walk through the door back into the diner. A waitress stands at our table, pouring coffee into a cup.

"We're not staying," Tommy says to her with a hard tone. I don't wait to hear her response; I walk out the front door, down the street to where Tommy parked the SUV.

"What happened, Kasia?" he asks as he straps me into my seat. I give a little shake of my head. I can't make my mouth work yet.

My door slams, then he's in the car. Once we're on the road, he pulls out his phone and makes a call.

If everything I read is right... No, I can't think of it. My stomach swirls again, just thinking it.

"I don't know. Just tell him to get home." Tommy's yelling into his phone.

I lean my head back against the seat.

"Then as soon as he can, dammit!" Tommy drops his phone into the middle console.

"Kasia." He touches my arm. "Are you sick? Do we need to go to the hospital?"

He pulls onto the expressway, heading west. We're leaving the city for home.

"No. I just want home," I say and close my eyes.

CHAPTER TWENTY

Dominik

By the time I get home the sun's already down. It's a clear night sky, but the black cloud hovering over my head as I run up the front steps of the house blocks it all out. Something's happened to Kasia. Tommy had no explanation that made any sense. All I know is he took her into her old neighborhood, and she ended up getting sick in a diner.

"Where is she?" I demand the moment Margaret appears. She's wringing her hands together and her lips are tight.

"Upstairs. She wouldn't come down. She wouldn't let me in the room," she says, her voice trailing behind me as I take the stairs two at a time.

Both Tommy and James are pacing outside the guestroom door.

"Boss." Tommy gets in front of me. "I swear, she was fine when she went into the bathroom."

"What happened, exactly?" I ask, resolving to keep my temper in check until I have a good reason to pound his face in. I've been away from the house more than I'd like, but she should have been safe. I pay these assholes to keep her safe.

"She wanted to get something to eat at this diner, so we went in. She went to the bathroom and I stayed at the booth. I kept an eye on the hallway where the bathrooms were, some guy went in and came back out a minute later. Nothing unusual for a guy taking a piss—"

"Talk faster, Tommy." My chest burns with the anger I'm holding back.

He blanches. "She didn't come right out, so I checked on her. When I went in, I found her in the stall, puking and clutching a bunch of papers to herself."

My ears perk. "Papers? What papers?"

"I don't know. She wouldn't let me see them. I got her out of there, to the car, then got hold of you. She's been in the room since we got back. Won't talk to anyone or let anyone in."

"You're sure she's in there?" I ask sarcastically.

His brow wrinkles. "I watched her. She went to the bathroom. Was I supposed to go in there with her?" he asks, getting defensive.

I set my jaw and stare him down until he takes a step back.

Turning to the door, I knock gently at first. "Kasia. It's me. Open the door," I say, knocking louder when I'm met with silence.

"Kasia. If you don't answer, I'm busting down the door," I warn, gesturing to Tommy to get the keys from downstairs.

There's a soft click and then the door pops open an inch. I push through into the room and shut the door behind me. The men don't need to hear our conversation.

When Kasia looks at me, rage fills me. Her eyes are swollen and red. The tip of her nose is tinged with pink. The woman has been up here sobbing herself sick.

"What's wrong?" I go to her, grabbing her shoulder, then checking her over. "Are you hurt? Are you sick?

Tommy said you were puking." I brush the hair that's stuck to her cheeks away from her face. Wet tears still linger on her skin.

"I'm not sick." She pushes my hands away.

"What happened, Kasia. What's wrong," I demand of her when she walks over to the bed and sits on the edge. Papers and photographs are strewn around the bed. When I get close, she leans over and wards me off with her hand.

"Don't touch anything." Her voice is low, angry.

I drag my hand through my hair. This isn't disobedience or defiance. This is something else, something stronger. Something I don't think is in her control.

"Tell me, then. What the fuck happened in that diner?" I stand in front of her, close enough to grab her, but I fold my arms over my chest, so she understands I won't.

"What did you find out when you talked with DeGrazio?" she asks me instead of giving me any information.

"Don't change the topic. Answer me." I need to know where her head is at.

She laughs, but it's joyless, empty. "No."

"Kasia."

"Fuck you, Dominik." She waves a hand through the air between us. It's a weak gesture. She's tired. "I knew you were a monster. I should have remembered. That first night. You kidnapped that guy's wife. I should have remembered." She taps her temple. "But I forgot because you…because you touch me and make me forget." There's an accusation there beneath her words.

"Kasia, you're making no sense."

I glance around the room. Aside from being angry, she's jumbling her words together. A bottle of brandy sits on her nightstand. No glass.

Leaning closer to her I can smell it. She reeks of it.

"How much have you had to drink?" I ask, picking up the bottle. It's not empty, but I don't know if she took an opened bottle or a new one.

"Not enough." Another sob breaks through her.

I reach for one of the photographs, but she hits my hand. I give her a hard glare, one that would have had her second thinking her actions yesterday, but she's brave now with the brandy. She holds my stare.

"You're drunk."

She laughs. "I wish." She picks up the photograph I was reaching for and hands it to me. "See this? That's my mom and my sister. They're dead." She drops the photograph as soon as I hold my hand out for it. "This one." She pushes documents away and finds another one and shoves it at me. "This one shows a train car. Do you see it?" She pushes it at me, so I take it.

As soon as my eyes make contact with the photo my blood pumps harder. I can hear it in my ears.

"My father…that's what he sells." She flicks a finger over the photograph of women chained together being hauled into a train car. This isn't new information to me, but obviously it is for her.

"Kasia."

"You knew though, right? I mean, you do business with him. That's what this marriage was about, settling some stupid territory argument?"

"Kasia, this isn't what I do." It's important that she understands this. I'm no fucking saint, but buying and selling women — we don't do that.

She lifts her eyes, her sad, tear-filled eyes to me.

"I don't believe you." The words are soft, but they hit me like a fucking freight train. "My father ordered that accident. He meant it to be me. I was supposed to get hit. And I was supposed to be taken." She picks up a crumbled piece of paper and shoves it at me.

Before I open it to read it, she tells me everything she knows.

"I was supposed to be taken to one of those trains. He was going to sell me, Dominik. He hired thugs to kidnap me and sell me." She sucks in a shaky breath and hugs herself around her middle.

That's not what the Kominski brothers told me. I pore over the document, hand scribbled notes from DeGrazio's meetings. I can't read most of it, names are coded, but what she's telling me is right. The deal was to have her taken to the trains on the south side. She was supposed to be sold.

"I knew he didn't love me. He blamed me because mom couldn't have any more kids after me."

"You're a twin, Kasia," I say stupidly. She's had more time to process all of this, I'm trying to catch up with her.

"I was the last out." She points to me. "There was a complication with my birth. Diana was already born. Easy peasy, but me...no. Something went wrong and although they saved my life, there was damage. Dad never got to have the son he wanted." She wipes the back of her hands across her face. "But sell me? Why? I was leaving for college in a year. I could have been gone from his life, why would..." she trails off, as though her brain just can't process the thought anymore.

"Where did you get all this?" I ask, gathering up everything from the bed. She's not paying me any attention anymore, so she doesn't get in my way.

"Degrazio."

"You promised me no more digging on your own." I stack the papers.

"Promised?" She laughs. "Fuck promises. Fuck everything. Nothing I did made that man like me. You know his favorite punishment was to keep Diana away from me? He didn't just take away my toys or ground me, he kept my sister away from me. He would take her out on vacations, day trips, dinners, whatever, while I was stuck at home. Alone."

I stare down at her. She's losing steam. The brandy is making her tired. She's run out of energy.

"When she died. It was my fault, I knew it, and he did too. He never let me forget it. But he didn't let me go. Why wouldn't he just let me leave if he hated me so much?" She lies down on the bed. "He should have just killed me."

It's at that my chest breaks open.

"No." I lean over her, brushing my fingertips over her jaw. "No, Kasia. He shouldn't have. He should have been a good father. He should have been a good man." He will pay for the evil he's done.

She shoves away my hand and rolls away from me. "Leave me alone, Dominik. Just leave me be."

I stare at her back. Her breathing is calm.

"Kasia." I touch her shoulder.

"I wish I had been in that car instead of Diana. I wish I had been the one who died."

My jaw tightens, my heart aches. A world without Kasia? I can't imagine it. I won't imagine it.

"Sleep, Kasia." I back away from the bed, taking everything DeGrazio gave her and grab her phone from the nightstand. I should move her to our room. She shouldn't be in this room anymore, but she's asleep now.

I turn off all the lights and step outside, closing the door behind me. Tommy and James stare at me.

"That fucker that went to the bathroom. He didn't go to the men's room." I point a finger at Tommy who has the smarts to avert his gaze. It's not his fault. Not really. There was no real danger in letting her go to the bathroom on her own. But my wife, my fucking world, is lying in that bed hurt because he didn't stop that fucker from giving her information she didn't need.

"Is she okay?" Tommy asks, guilt dripping from his tone.

"No." I pinch the bridge of my nose. "It's not…he didn't hurt her. He's the private investigator I told never to contact her again. But he did. The Kominski brothers fucking lied to me." I close my eyes for a brief moment.

I'd finally gotten good news from my father's attorney today. I was about to call him and arrange for him to return home, but that's not at the forefront of my mind now.

"I want a sit down with Kominski. Not his fucking sons.

Him!" I bark. I point at James. "You stay here. If she tries to leave, you call me. She can go to our bedroom or she stays in there. She goes nowhere else."

"You got it, boss," he says with a nod and stands right in front of the door.

Tommy hurries ahead of me, already on the phone to get the old man ready for my visit. I'm not waiting until morning. I want that fucker to tell me to my face what the fuck the deal actually was.

CHAPTER TWENTY-ONE

Kasia

Not even the shower is helping my sore muscles and throbbing head. The brandy didn't help as much as I hoped it would. It only made things foggier. I don't remember everything from the night before. I do remember Dominik coming into the room.

I remember the anger in my heart and the concern on his face.

It's too much to think about right now. I turn off the water and dry off, taking it slow. All the damn crying has made me tired still. My entire life, I'd kept from crying like that because of my father. But after seeing what he had planned. What he had wanted to do to me, it's like a dam burst inside me that I couldn't stop.

All of my clothes have been moved to Dominik's bedroom, so I put my sundress back on from yesterday. I'm not up for seeing him yet. He must be so angry with me for meeting with Degrazio behind his back. Tommy called him home after he found me in the bathroom at the diner. I'm proving to be more trouble than I'm worth, I'm sure.

My phone's gone, as well as everything DeGrazio gave

me. Dominik must have all of it.

When I open the door, one of Dominik's men I haven't met yet greets me.

"Hello, Mrs. Staszek. Your husband has left orders for you to either stay in this room or go to your room."

I stare at him. He means Dominik's room.

"Am I not allowed food?" I ask, trying to hide my snark. It's my own fault this is happening. I've stayed in my room, hiding away from everything all day long. Dominik is probably contemplating how to deal with me, his errant, stupid, worth-nothing wife.

"You mean dinner? Of course. I'll ask Margaret to bring up something," he says, pulling his phone out of his pocket. Apparently, I'm not to be left alone even for the short time it would take for him to go downstairs.

I touch his arm before he finishes dialing. "No, that's okay. Thanks. I'll just go to Dominik's room." I walk past him and go to the next room so I can change into clean clothes.

The last of the afternoon sun shines through the window, making the pain in my head even sharper. I close the blinds and quickly change. I'm not spending any more time locked away. I don't care what Dominik does to me, or what his men threaten. I'm tired of being hidden and imprisoned.

With fresh clothes on, I open the bedroom door. The same soldier stands there waiting for me to ask him to do something for me. I don't need him to do anything. I'll take care of myself.

"I need to use the car." I step out of the room and into the hall.

He squares off with me, his brows pulled together with worry. He's probably not sure what to do. Does he drag me back in the room, does he call for help? Seeing as he's unsure, I'm positive Dominik's not in the house.

Good.

That makes things easier.

"Your husband said—"

"Yeah. I heard you the first time. It doesn't change that I need the car. You have two choices here. You can get out of my way so I can go, or you can come with me in case there's trouble." I don't really want him with me, but I'm also not stupid enough to think I'll get far without one of his men at least following me. Besides, maybe he'll come in handy. He does have a gun after all.

His gaze darts past me to the stairs. His options are limited, and I've put him a tough spot.

I don't care.

Right now, I only care about getting what I want. It's worked for my father in the past, it works for Dominik every day. Demand what you want, and if it's not handed to you — just fucking take it.

"Where do you want to go?" Defeat dances in his question.

"I'm driving." I turn on my heel and head to the stairs. He's right behind me, already starting to try and talk me out of it.

"I'm going to have to call Dominik," he says just as I reach the garage door. It gives me a moment of pause. I don't want him fucking this up for me.

"Fine. Once we're in the car and have cleared the gates, you can call him and tattle. But if you call him before that…" I shrug and pull the garage door open.

"Kasia? Is that you?" Margaret's voice trails down the hallway. Damn this house. Gorgeous, yes, but all the openness makes it damn near difficult to sneak away.

I don't say a word to her. Instead I walk across the three-car garage and climb into the black SUV. I don't have my purse or my wallet, but it's not like I'm not driving without protection. If a cop pulls us over, soldier boy will have to get us out of trouble.

He climbs in beside me, his phone already cradled in his hands.

"It's a push start," he says, and drops the fob in the

cupholder of the center console.

Once the garage door opens, I pull out quickly and head to the gate.

"What's your name?" I ask him as he taps on his screen. The gate closes behind us and I turn onto the main street that will take us right to the expressway.

"Michael," he mutters and puts the phone to his ear.

The expressway is clear while we're still in the suburbs, but the closer to the city we get I know I'm going to run into traffic.

"Boss, she's out of the house. I'm with her...I don't know, she won't say..." He presses a button on the touch screen of the car and Dominik's voice booms through the car.

"Kasia, what the hell are you doing?" he demands.

"Taking care of some things," I answer. His general answers have been good enough for him to give me, it's about time he was treated the same.

"Go back to the house. Michael is going to take you home."

"No." I change lanes and speed up, merging onto the highway. "I'll be home sometime after dinner. Don't wait for me." I glance at the console and hang up the call.

I can feel Michael's panic roll off of him.

"Don't worry. He'll survive."

"Yeah," he mutters. "It's me I'm worried about."

I smile at that.

It takes over an hour to get to my father's house. I'm told he's out of town, but I'm not really looking for him, so it won't matter.

"Jesus, why are we here?" he asks, as I pull up to the curb. My father's house isn't a gated estate like Dominik's. No armed guards walking the property.

"You can call your boss again if it will make you feel better. We aren't going to be long." I grab the fob so he can't withhold it from me and hop down from the car.

The front door is still controlled by a keypad, and

thankfully my father never saw fit to change the code after he sold me to Dominik. The house is quiet. Dad's office is open.

It's not as scary now that it's empty. Now that I'm an adult who has finally grabbed the reins of my own life.

"Kasia, what are we doing here?" Michael asks in a hushed whisper. His hand is posed on the butt of his gun.

"Don't worry. He's gone." I sit at Dad's desk and open the filing cabinet drawer. I thumb through the files until I find the one I'm looking for.

"Dominik will be here soon," he tells me, like an annoying big brother who's informed our father I'm snooping.

I get the address I need and stuff the file back into the drawer.

"Good for him." I slam the drawer and get up. I walk right past him and down the hall, not sparing a glance at the family pictures hanging on the wall. I'm not in most of them and if I am, I'm tucked off to the side.

Fuck them.

Fuck everything here.

When I climb back into the SUV, Michael is right next to me.

"Tell me where we're going," he demands. He could end this right now and grab me, but I know he won't. He's young and hasn't been around Dominik enough to know that stopping me by any means is probably safer for him than letting me do what I'm about to do.

"Making things right," I say and pull away from the house. He grabs onto the handle of the door. I'll admit my driving is a bit erratic, but there are lives at stake. I can't wait around for men to decide to stop being monsters.

"Kasia. Where are you headed?" Dominik's voice comes through the car speakers again. Michael called him again, I suppose.

"The transports leave every Thursday night." I remember from hearing my father talking about them. I assumed he was moving stolen cars or merchandise, not people. I never thought he could be so cruel. I was an idiot.

"Kasia. Pull the car over. I'll be there within ten minutes," he orders.

"Sorry, I can't."

"Kasia, do what I'm telling you right now." There's worry laced in his demand.

"Do you want to threaten me with a spanking, Dominik?" I switch lanes, heading south.

"Kasia. I swear to you, it will so much worse than that if you don't do as I tell you, right now."

He's bluffing. Maybe he's not. I don't really care anymore.

"Bye, Dominik." I hang up again and find the button that disconnects the bluetooth. "Call him again, Michael, and you'll be walking home," I say in Polish to be sure he gets my meaning clearly, and head for the next exit.

The sun is gone now, night has settled around us. This isn't exactly the best part of Chicago, so it would be best if Michael, and his gun, stayed with me.

CHAPTER TWENTY-TWO

Kasia

There isn't exactly a directory posted at the train yard, but I remember this place. My father took Diana and I here when we were kids. He let us play on the empty train car while he talked with men in suits. They talked too fast for me to understand them. My Polish wasn't as good then.

A quick look around the car and I find what I need. A gun is hidden in the middle console.

"You may want to draw your weapon," I say to Michael as we climb out of the SUV. We'll have to walk down several rows of cars before we get to the place my father took me.

"This isn't a good idea. Let's wait for Dominik to get here," he says.

I pause a moment, then realize my error. "There's GPS in the car. He knows exactly where we are."

"So maybe we should wait," he urges me but keeps his voice low.

There's a sound up ahead that makes me stop. I put a finger over my lips to keep him quiet too. He looks at me like I've lost my mind. He's probably done this a million times and doesn't need me to explain to be quiet.

"Almost loaded, Marcin." I hear a familiar voice carry to me. The car's already loaded on the tracks.

I wave Michael to follow me and run toward the sound.

"Don't forget the fucking water this time. Last week two of them nearly fucking died. I had to take half price on them." My father's voice booms. He's not even trying to maintain a low profile. But why would he?

I look over at Michael, at the gun in his hands, then at the one in mine. I've never fired one before. I swallow, fear claws at my throat. No matter what I think I know what I'm going to find, it could be worse.

There's never been much love between my father and myself, but I've always thought him decent. As good as a man in his position could be, but now, I'm being faced with a horror that was meant for me. A terrifying scene that he'd planned for me.

"Kasia." Michael's whisper shakes me from my thoughts. "What are you hoping to accomplish here? Your father has many men here. There's just us. Let's wait for Dominik. He'll have others with him."

It's a sound plan. But I'm tired of waiting for backup. It's never come before, and it's not going to start now. My father wanted me to grow up alone, he sent me with a man who would keep me in solitude. I won't cow to it. I can be strong all on my own.

He curses when I move forward. I won't be talked out of this. When I get to the next row, I press myself against the car before looking around the corner.

What I see twists my stomach.

Women tethered together at the ankles and hands stand at the bottom of a ramp leading into the open train car on the tracks. They're dirty, their clothes are tattered, and they're scared. Their muffled sobs tear at my heart. Not even the gags in their mouths are helping to keep them silent. This was meant for me. That was to be my future.

Tears prick my eyes, but I dash them away. There's no time for that.

"Kasia—"

"No." I put my hand up in Michael's face. "No more." I glance back at the women. My father is walking around the five of them huddled together. The moonlight strikes his face and for a moment I can see his features. How pleased he is with his capture.

"Come with me or don't. That's your decision." I cock the gun and take a deep breath. "I've already made mine."

He calls for me again, but I'm already walking toward them, toward my father, those women.

"Tata!" I call out to him. He freezes like he's been struck in the back. When he turns toward me, two of his men flank him, weapons drawn and pointed at me. That's fine, mine is aimed at him.

"Kasia?" He squints, the darkness probably makes it hard for him to see me. "What are you doing here?" he demands. "You little fool. Is your husband here?" He looks past me, but there's only Michael. I can feel him close to me.

"This is what you wanted for me?" I stop several feet from him. The women huddle closer together. "You wanted to put me on this train? Where's it going, anyway?"

"Who told you this?" he asks. His hands fidget at his sides. "Who lies to you? Your husband? The Staszek asshole?"

My insides shake. "You sent the Kominski family to take me, to steal me away so you could sell me." I can't seem to get the volume in my voice to match the rage in my chest.

"Kłamać!" *Lies.*

"It was supposed to be me in that car, how many times over the years did you remind me? Me! But you didn't want me dead…you wanted me here. Tied up like this, taken away and sold." My voice breaks toward the end, but I can't help it. Tears build in my eyes. This is my father. My dad. The man who taught me to ride a bike when I was little. The man who once held my hand as we crossed the street.

Before it was confirmed my mother could never get pregnant again, he held some tenderness for me. He was kind. That's the father I've been holding in my heart. But this man standing here, looking disgusted by my presence. This isn't him.

I raise my gun higher, pointing it at his head.

"What? You think you can pull the trigger? You're a badass now?" He taunts me, raising his square chin. "Go on. Show me what a bad ass you are."

A tear falls down my cheek. Why can't I be steady? Why can't I tug on this fucking trigger? He deserves worse, he deserves to burn in hell.

"Why?" The question leaves me on a breath. "Why do this when you could have just let me leave?"

"Leave?" His brows raise. "You wouldn't leave. You'd come back, you'd always be there, always need me. You'd always be a spot on my family name. You needed to go away."

"You could have just killed me." A sharp pain hits me. I knew he didn't love me, but this, this look of disgust squeezes my heart.

"You were worth more alive." His lips twist into a disturbing grin.

"Ah, but *you* aren't, Garska." Dominik's voice booms from behind me. Tension eases in my shoulders, but I don't lower my gun. This is for me to end. Not him.

"What are you talking about?" Dad sneers. "Zabij ich!" *Kill them!*

I swing my gun to the left of my father, to his men, and pull the trigger. One yelps, but doesn't go down. I think I've hit his shoulder. Dominik rages behind me, grabbing me and shoving me backward. It takes only a second for him to pick off the two guards. One shot to the one I wounded, then one to the second man. They both crumble to the ground.

My father looks behind him. The women are in a panic, screaming behind their gags.

"Where is everyone! Come! Come!" my father yells.

Dominik stalks up to him, his gun lowered. "Your men

have been taken care of," he says, coming toe to toe with him.

"Dominik!" I yell. He doesn't turn away from my father. "He's…let me," I say still holding my gun up.

"Michael, take this prick over there for now. If he moves, shoot his cock off." Dominik grabs my father by the collar and shoves him toward Michael who is already making his way to him.

I want to demand they stop moving. To stop taking over this moment from me, but I can't get the words out. My hands shake so hard, I'm not sure I'd even hit my target.

I lower the gun and run to the plank leading to the train car. I need to see. I need to know how many there are.

Air escapes me. The car is nearly full. More than twenty women. All tied together with rope, all dirty, their gags are around their necks. Some have been beaten. Others injured in other ways. All of them look back at me with terrified eyes.

I cover my mouth, unable to bear the horror. A few of the girls are barely teenagers.

"I'll get you out," I promise them as I run to the closest woman and tug on the knots. I need a knife. "I'm sorry…so sorry." I'm sobbing and tugging on their restraints.

"Kasia." Dominik enters the car. "Kasia."

It's not until he touches me that I realize I'm not moving anymore. He turns me to face him, brings up my chin.

"They're hurt," I say, a numbness starting to cloud me.

"They will be taken care of. I promise." He holds my face in his hands. "Are you hurt?"

"He wanted this for me." I blink, tears stream down my cheeks.

"He won't hurt you ever again." His jaw clenches.

"I didn't listen to you. I came without you." My mind wanders like the breeze.

He presses his forehead to mine, breathing deeply and wrapping his hands around the back of my neck.

"These girls. They need…why would he…and you…I

know you wouldn't…"

"Shhhh." He lifts away from me, leveling me with his arrogant stare. "What do you need, Kasia? How do I help? What do you want me to do?"

It takes a few seconds for the words to sink in. He's asking me for directions. Me, his wife.

"We have to help these women," I say firmly. "We can't let this go unpunished."

"Your father." He nods. "There's been a decision on that that even I can't disobey."

I can't imagine there being a higher power than him, but I know how these things work. At least in generalities. He answers to his father, and his father answers to the families at the highest ranks.

"Do you want to say anything to him?"

"No." I look at the women. They aren't huddled anymore. No one says anything. They're probably too afraid.

Dominik gestures to one of his men at the entrance of the car. I can't make out who it is before he jogs down the ramp and out of sight.

Dominik pulls me to his chest, he wraps his arms around my body, then one around my head. I can't breathe very well, it's too tight, but then I hear it.

A single shot. Muffled, but I know it for what it is.

My father's dead.

If Dominik wasn't holding me up, I'm not sure I'd stay on my feet.

When he unravels me from his arms, he kisses my forehead. It's tender, sweet, nothing like him, but exactly what I needed.

"My men will help these women. We need to leave now, though," he says to me, softly.

"They aren't to be mistreated, Dominik."

"They won't be. I swear it, Kasia." He brings my hand to his chest. "So long as my heart beats, I will never lie to you."

I swallow back another sob. The night has been too much. All the strength I had when I started out has waned away, leaving me a mess.

"I think I want to go home, Dominik."

Silently, he takes my hand and leads me from the car. His men are already inside untying the women, speaking softly to them, being careful. The women that witnessed my exchange with my father watch me as I walk past them. They rub their wrists that are no longer bound.

"Thank you," one says, then another.

"I am so sorry this was done to you," I say to them. Dominik tugs me along before I can say more.

Two of Dominik's men drag something heavy behind them, away from the car. A body. My father.

Dominik won't let me stop; he tugs me along. Shouldn't I feel something? I can't untangle everything running through my mind.

By the time we get to the car, Tommy's already there, holding the back door open. Dominik helps me inside. He says something to Tommy then climbs in next to me.

My family is dead.

All of them, gone.

I'm all alone.

CHAPTER TWENTY-THREE

Dominik

It's a fucking mess.

Marcin Garska was moving twenty-five girls in that train car. Even for a prick like him, that's ambitious. We were able to get information from one of his men before he was tossed in a death pile. The car was headed east to New York. From there it would have been put on a boat headed for Russia.

Garska wasn't even doing business with our own people. He was bringing the fucking Bratva into the mix.

Fucking prick.

The women have all been moved to a hotel nearby. We've rented the whole floor, and my men are keeping them safe.

It's been a full day since the shit storm began, and Kasia is avoiding me. But that has to end. I can't let her sink too far into her own darkness. We may never find each other again if we do that.

"She had some lunch," Margaret informs me when I walk into the kitchen. I see the empty plate in her hands.

"Good." I look out into the yard, toward her tree. The

sun is beating down hard today, she won't be in the rose garden.

Kasia sits in her chair, her knees pulled up to her chest and her chin resting on her knee. If she folds herself any further into herself, she'll disappear altogether.

"Boss." Tommy walks into the kitchen. "There's a cop at the door." He looks out at Kasia. "Her father's been found."

We were expecting it. It's better for Kasia if he's off the books.

I follow Tommy to the front door. A uniformed cop and a suited-up detective stand on my porch. I know the detective.

"Mr. Staszek. We're hoping to talk with your wife, Kasia? This concerns her father."

"My wife isn't feeling well. You can tell me what you need to," I say, folding my arms over my chest. Asking her to pretend as though she doesn't already know her father's dead is too much. She's in pain already, I won't add to it.

"We need to notify the next of kin." The cop keeps his features schooled.

Detective Stevenson clears his throat. "It'll all right. We can give the information to Mr. Staszek. If his wife has questions, she can reach out to me personally." His eyes fix on me. He'll want a boost in his next payment.

The uniformed cop frowns but gives me the news. Marcin Garska was found dead in his own train car, apparent suicide. I nod along as he speaks, not interrupting him while he tells me when and how we can get his body for burial. He can burn for all I care, but Kasia may want to give him a proper funeral.

It's up to her.

"Thank you," I say once they're all done. "We'll be in touch if we need anything." I shut the door before the detective can make a show of handing me a card.

"Was that about Dad?" Kasia is behind me when I shut the door.

"Yeah." I bolt the door and turn to her. "We can pick up his remains in two days, once they do...well, what they do." I'm not going into details. She doesn't need those images in her mind.

Her hair is pulled into a messy ponytail at the base of her neck, her eyes puffy from crying, and there's red blotches on her cheeks. I step toward her, and she takes one back.

"Kasia."

She shakes her head. "I...I've never planned a funeral before." She wraps her arms around her stomach.

"I can have it taken care of. Just tell me what you want. What you need." Seeing her this way, the pain clearly etched on her face, the heartbreak evident in her voice — it makes me want to put another bullet in Marcin's fucking head.

"I don't have family...he was it. An uncle, but he's still in Poland. He never moved here." She raises her eyes to mine. "I don't want him buried next to my mother or sister. He doesn't get to spend eternity with them."

I nod, what else can I do? I need to wipe away her pain. "He won't be."

"He has friends, business associates. They will probably expect something," she blows out air. Just this little bit of an interaction is taking too much energy.

"A small service. He'll be cremated and the ashes will be sent back to Poland, to his brother. He can figure out what to do with him. Is that all right?"

I take another step toward her, and she stands firm this time.

"Yes. That sounds...good," she frowns. There's nothing good in this situation. "The women from last night."

"They are staying at the Hilton on Ogden. They're being protected and I'm having two doctors head over there this afternoon to help anyone who needs it. A few girls needed immediate care last night, it's been taken care of." I feel like I'm making a report to my boss. If she doesn't approve, she'll slip further away. I can feel her sliding away from me.

"What will happen to them now?" she asks, raising her

chin.

"I don't know, Kasia. From what I'm told, some of them have been sold and bought three times over. The girls that want to go home can be taken home whenever they are ready, but the others…some of them don't have anywhere to go."

Her frown deepens. "They have no one," she whispers. "Like me."

"No." I cringe at the force in my voice, but I can't help it. "You're not like them at all. You're not alone." I grab her arms, keeping her from running up the stairs. She looks like she wants to run. "You're here with me. You have me."

"You have everything now, Dominik. You don't need me anymore. My dad's gone; you'll get to take his territories." Her shoulders sag.

I stare at her a long moment. Remembering the panic overtaking me as I made my way to her yesterday. How I couldn't look away from the GPS tracking to be sure I knew where she was, how I could get to her. I remember the cold fear of seeing Marcin's men's guns aimed at her when I found them. If they demanded I hand over everything to keep her safe, I would have. It wouldn't have taken even a blink of an eye to agree.

"I already have everything, Kasia." A tear slides down her cheek, and I catch it with my thumb, wiping it away. "You. I have everything because I have you."

There's a tremble in her lower lip.

"Do you hear me? You are everything I need." I grip her tighter. "Tell me I haven't lost you because of this, tell me you're not gone from me," I demand.

She brings her hands up and wraps them around my wrist. Not to tear me away from her, but to touch me. To put a connection between us.

"You're not my father," she says quietly. "Even in your most asshole moods, you've never made me feel unnecessary."

I should have been the one to put that bullet in Marcin's

head. Maybe I wouldn't feel so much anger toward him still. "I promise, Kasia, I swear on my mother's grave, I will never allow anyone to hurt you again. You will never feel alone, never be without love again. Never." It's a vow I feel more sincerely than the ones I muttered in that damn chapel weeks ago.

Was it that short of a time ago? It feels like Kasia has been in my life for longer, much longer. Maybe because she takes up so much of my life now.

There's purpose to me now. Not just work, but her. She's my point.

"I'm sorry I took off like that," she says after a long silence stretches between us. "I should have waited for you. I thought...I was afraid you wouldn't let me go."

"I wouldn't have," I say honestly. "I would have tied you to my bed to keep you from going there to see what you saw. To have that horror etched into your mind."

"When you got there, you didn't order your men to take me away. You asked me what I wanted done." She seems confused by this still. Doesn't she understand?

"I will always be there, always ready to stand in front of you to protect you, and to stand behind you when you need support." I press my forehead to hers. "Kocham Cię, Kasia." *I love you.*

"Kocham Cię, Dominik."

It's the first time I've heard her speak in Polish, and I will always remember it.

I kiss her, not one of ownership or power, but a tender kiss that relays every emotion I hold for her. I went into this marriage as a way to help my father, a way to expand our territory. But I've gotten so much more.

I have Kasia.

CHAPTER TWENTY-FOUR

Kasia

It's past nine o'clock when Dominik comes up to our bedroom. He sent me up here after dinner to *think* about what was going to happen when he came up.

My father's service was two weeks ago. His ashes have probably already reached his brother in Poland. I met with his attorney this afternoon and signed all the paperwork to claim my inheritance. My father never wanted me to have anything, but he never changed his will. I get everything.

I want none of it.

Instead I've instructed my father's attorney to sell everything that can be sold. Once everything's liquidated, Dominik has agreed to help me build a halfway house for women. I know his family doesn't sell women, but that doesn't mean it's not happening.

Every woman we saved that night has been brought home or are being set up with a new life. That's why the halfway house is needed. They need a safe place to stay while they get an education, find new footing in this world. I may not be using my education degree to teach young minds, but I will be using my skills to help people who need a helping hand.

And yet...I'm sitting in our bedroom, waiting for my husband to come upstairs to punish me.

He mentioned something about getting too big for my britches. My grandmother used to use that term. It's old school, but if I know anything about my husband, it's how traditional he is. And he doesn't like it when his wife starts ordering him about in front of his men. And I suppose outright defying him when he told me to stay out of the sun this afternoon wasn't the right move either.

If he thought having me worry about the punishment was going to make it worse, he was mistaken. He won't spank me, that will be sad because I do love it when he brings a hot hum to my body, but he'll use pleasure against me. I'm not worried.

The bedroom door opens, and Dominik walks inside with a tight expression. He's been home most of the day, so he's not wearing his suit. He's in a casual t-shirt and black jeans. His feet are bare.

I stand up from the bed, drop my robe to the floor at my feet. It's a challenge.

He raises his left eyebrow.

"Obviously, I've been too lenient with you over these past weeks." He heads straight for the closet and jerks the door open. He's been wonderful these past weeks. I've seen a new side of him, tender and passionate. But I miss the other part of him, the tense, arrogant, stubborn dominant part of him.

There's a stick in his hand when he reemerges from the closet.

"What's that for?" I give a pointed look to his hand.

"Oh this?" He waves it in the air, creating a sharp swishing sound. "It's a cane, Kasia."

I back up a pace until my legs hit the bed. "A cane?"

"Yep." He stalks to me, kicking my robe out of the way. "You've been a big talker these past few days." He presses the tip of the cane to my chin, pushing it up until my head is back and I have to look down the length of my nose at him.

"I was…I mean…" I shrug. "Sorry?"

He breaks into a wide grin, but the resolve is still there. "Not yet, but you will be, Kasia. I promise. Turn around and put your hands flat on the bed. Stick your ass out."

"You're sure you don't want to do that thing with the vibrator again?" I ask. I'm walking the line, teasing him like this, but my nerves have started acting up. I've never had the cane used on me. His belt feels good, his hand is amazing, and the flogger he used last week sent me flying fast. But this beast doesn't look like it will do anything other than hurt.

"No, no. This is better for a naughty girl like you. A few stripes across your ass and you'll be ready for the rest of your punishment."

"Rest?"

"This is just the beginning. Now turn around, bad girl." He taps the cane to my cheek then walks back a few steps to give me room to get in position.

With a shaky stomach, I do what he says. It's not going to be so bad. Dominik won't do anything that I can't survive.

"Keep your hands out of my way, keep your feet planted, and unless you're going to thank me, don't open your mouth. Understood?" He presses the length of the cane against my ass.

It won't be bad.

"Yes. I understand." I fist my hands, just in case.

The first strike sends my brain rocketing into orbit. I'm off the bed, jumping up and down, grabbing my ass. Fuck!

"Couldn't even be good for the first stroke." He shakes his head sadly, but I can see his cock pressing against his jeans. He's not entirely unhappy about all this. "Back in position. Now I have to start over."

I take a deep breath and go back over the bed. I'll do it better. He won't get the better of me.

The second stroke makes me scream, but I keep my feet planted.

He runs the cane over the line of fire the last stroke made.

"Bad girls don't get to have orgasms, isn't that right?" He turns the cane and runs it between my legs, up through my wet sex. Fuck, I already want him, and it's only been two strokes.

"That's right." I clench my teeth.

"Hmmm, I think tonight will be different." A drawer opens and closes and then he drops a small vibrator on my hand. "Tonight, you'll practice obedience. Use that toy to make yourself come for me, Kasia."

I look over my shoulder; he's still holding the cane.

"Do you need that?" I ask him.

He smiles. "Oh definitely."

He's playful. That's never a good thing when he's trying to punish me.

"Dominik. I'm sorry if I've been rude."

"No." He shakes his head. "I don't want your apology yet. I'll let you know when. Now get to work." He uses the cane to point to the vibrator.

I sigh and pick it up. After I switch it on, I place it over my clit. The vibrations right away kick up my arousal, the fact that he's watching only heightens my need.

Just as I start to care more about the good sensation than his eyes lingering on me, he brings the cane down on my ass. I jolt forward, my brain screeches to a halt.

"Carry on," he says.

I clench my jaw and get back to it, chasing down the pleasure before he can take it away from me, but as soon as my body tightens, the cane comes down again, and again.

I growl. It's distracting having both happening at the same time.

"Keep going." He taps the cane to my ass.

This time I'm careful to hide my expression. I get close, so close to the first burst of release when the cane comes down sharply, harder than the others across my ass. I cry out, but I don't move the vibrator away. I'm too close to stop now. He brings the cane down again, but I'm lost to the waves.

The sharp strike of the cane melds into the haze of my orgasm, and there's no separation between them. I'm all wrapped up in both sensations, being carried off with them. I collapse forward on the bed, humping the vibrator harder as his hands grab my hips.

"Don't stop," he orders and the cane lands on the bed beside my head. He unzips his pants and presses the length of his cock between my ass cheeks.

Instinct makes my body tense. I clench every muscle.

"Don't tighten up, Kasia, it will only make this next part more uncomfortable." His thumb swipes through my wet folds, pushing the vibrator out of the way as he gathers up my own juices to use against me. He's good at this, at making my desire a punishment.

"Dominik," I reach behind and grasp his wrist. He's fingered me there before, but never has his cock pierced my asshole.

He shakes off my hand and smacks my ass, sending a ripple of fire through my body.

"Don't reach back here again. Keep that vibrator on your clit." He smears my juices across my asshole, then presses the tip of his cock against my tight ring of muscle. I clench my eyes, and everything else. "Relax, Kasia. I'm fucking your ass with or without your help. Either this hurts a lot or not too bad. Your choice." He pulls my ass cheeks apart and presses harder against me. The round head of his cock intrudes, breaking through the muscle.

"Fuck!" I yell, fisting my hand and pressing my face into the bed. I can't do it. It burns, so much heat.

"Deep breath." He thrusts further, the pain increases, but I do what he says. I suck in a hot breath and force my body to soften. If I don't fight him, if I give over, it will be easier. It might be good. It's the same with him. When I charge at him, he's a brick wall — unmovable.

"Fuck, Kasia." He moans behind me as his cock inches further. Tears escape my clenched lids. "So tight." He reaches around me, taking the vibrator from me and pressing it harder against my body.

Vibrations blossom new arousal.

"Dominik," I whisper his name, though I'm not sure what I want from him. I don't want him to stop, that I know, that I won't tell him.

"Such a good girl, taking my cock up your ass." He thrusts harder. "Take all of me." His order is overpowered by his final push. Completely embedded in my ass, I can't believe how full I feel. How hot and needy I am for him.

"Please," I cry when the vibrator passes over my clit again. I arch my back, pushing my ass back at him. He's a rough man, an impossible man, and it's his power I crave now. I need all of it, the parts that hurt, the parts that soothe. Every bit of it sets my body on fire. An inferno only he can extinguish.

"Who owns you, Kasia?" He plows into me hard. The stripes from the cane sting, pushing me to another level of desire.

"You do, Dominik." And I mean it. I can't imagine being with anyone else. Giving myself this way to anyone else.

"Are you going to be good now?" Another hard thrust and my ass clings around his shaft, stretching to fit him into me.

If he'll keep fucking me like this the rest of my life, I'll vow obedience every single night.

"Yes!" There's another orgasm rising. The vibrator rubs against my clit while his cock fills me.

He shoves hard into me. "Do you think you deserve to come again?"

"Yes. Please, Dominik. I'm sorry. I'll be good. I promise!"

He growls behind me, his body doing all the talking now. "Kasia." My name is all the permission I need.

When the bubble inside me bursts, I hold nothing back. He doesn't slow, he doesn't give me time to adjust to the harsh waves of pleasure sucking the breath out of me. He fucks me even harder, chasing after his own release.

My hips hurt when his nails dig into my skin as he's carried away with his own orgasm. He groans, yelling out my name once, then stills behind me.

The room is silent. Except for the hum of the vibrator. He switches the little bullet off and tosses it toward the pillows.

Dominik smacks my ass as he pulls free of my body. I clench my asshole, not wanting his seed to drip down my legs.

"Go slow," he says. The tenderness has returned to his voice. "Are you hurt?" With a feathery touch his fingertips touch my ass cheek.

"No," I'm quick to assure him.

He grunts. "I went too easy on you, then."

Gingerly, I climb up into bed, under the covers and wait for him.

He finishes shucking off his clothes and tosses the cane to the floor. The bed dips when he climbs beneath the covers. After flicking the light off, he gathers me up in his arms and holds me tight to his chest. A chaste kiss is pressed to my forehead.

"Kasia. My family will be here soon. When my father's here, you have to behave." I hear the warning. He's let me off easy tonight; he won't be so tolerant when his family is around.

"You want to put on a show of strength for your dad?"

"No. I want him to see you for what you are, and this little brat you've been playing at this past week isn't you." He hugs me tighter.

He's not wrong. "I don't know what's gotten into me."

"I do," he says. "I've been too sweet, given you too much room to wander around alone. So, you act out. You're not fragile, Kasia. And I'm going to stop treating you like you are."

"I've missed you, this part of you anyway." I say into the darkness, snuggling into his chest.

"You won't have to miss me anymore. There's a lot of work to do, for both of us. And together we can do it all."

It warms me to hear him talk this way. There's no more him and me, it's always us. We're together.

"I love you, Dominik." I yawn.

"I love you, too, Kasia." He kisses my head again. "Now, get some sleep before I have to pick up the cane and we start all over again."

I laugh, but he pinches where a welt is forming from the cane.

"All right. I get your point."

"Good girl."

CHAPTER TWENTY-FIVE

Dominik
A month later...

Kasia's a bundle of nerves, pacing around the house looking for something to do. Margaret's already kicked her out of the kitchen twice.

"Kasia. You are going to wear a hole in the living room," I say, not looking up from my phone.

"I wish Margaret would let me do something. I hate having nothing to do but wait."

My father and sister are coming over for dinner. They've been home for a few days, but Kasia has been so busy with the halfway house, I suggested we wait for the weekend.

"Aren't they here yet?" Jakub saunters into the living room with a palm full of black olives. He pops one into his mouth then peeks out the front window.

"They will get here when they get here." I shake my head. Not an ounce of patience between the two of them. And the most impulsive one, my sister, hasn't even arrived yet.

"What if your sister doesn't like me?" Kasia whispers to me, glancing over to be sure Jakub can't hear her. All the drama in our lives has kept her and Jakub from really getting to know each other, but things are settling now. As much as life in my world can calm.

"My sister? What about my dad?"

She scrunches up her face and blows off the idea. "No. If your sister doesn't like me, it's a bigger problem. Trust me."

I roll my eyes. Lena can be petty. She's definitely spoiled and stubborn, but she won't cause trouble for Kasia and me. She'll be happy for us.

"Here they are." Jakub tosses the last olive into his mouth and heads to the door.

I glance at Kasia then stuff my phone in my jeans. "Relax. They will love you. And if they don't, they'll keep it to themselves." Or they'll face me.

My comment doesn't relax her.

I grab her hand and we go to the door together. When I pull it open, I see my father making his way up the front steps. He's alone. His driver is already back in the car pulling away to park in the garage.

"Where's Lena?" I ask.

My father looks to me, his eyes widen. "She's not here?"

My stomach falls. "Why would she be here? Didn't she come with you?"

"She went out with friends this morning, said she'd meet me here," my father explains. He pulls out his phone and shows me her message.

I read the text.

Going to Dom's on my own. See you there.

I hand the phone back. "Well, let's get inside then we'll call her," I say. "You should meet Kasia first, though." I take her hand and squeeze.

"Mr. Staszek," she smiles at him.

He looks her over then grins. "My son tells me you're nothing like your old man." He nods. "That's good."

She tightens her hold on me but keeps quiet. I'll talk to him later about being an ass.

"I'm kidding." He pulls her into him for a big hug. No matter what an asshole the man is on the streets, when it comes to his family, he's always been a bit of a softy. At least where the women were concerned. "I'm glad to have you in the family. Dominik says only kind things about you. And as big of an asshole he may be, he's an honest asshole," he says with another laugh.

While they make small talk, I call Lena. The call goes to voicemail.

"She texted you instead of talking to you at home?"

"I told you, she went out with her friends. I got her text while I was changing my shoes." He points at his new loafers. The man loves his shoes the way some men enjoy cars.

"You didn't text her back or call her?" I demand. He's too permissive with her.

"She said she'll be here. She'll be here. It's not like she isn't old enough to have her own plans," Dad argues. "I'm hungry." He looks to Kasia. "Did you eat lunch yet?"

Kasia gives me a quick glance then steps toward the kitchen. "No, we were waiting for you." She disappears into the kitchen with my father and brother following after her.

I look down at my phone again.

Lena was born in Chicago. All of her friends are here. Maybe she just wanted to go out for a bit before she came over, or she wanted to have her own ride so she could duck out in time to meet up with friends.

I tell myself all of this as I head to the kitchen, but there's a sinking sensation in my stomach that nags me.

"Dominik," my dad says from next to Kasia at the kitchen island. "Don't worry. Your sister's just being a pain in the ass again. She'll be here soon. Come. Let's eat. I'm starving. Then we can talk business."

I watch Kasia talk with my father like she's known him for years. He's already at ease around her. She's good with that. Making people feel important. Making them feel wanted.

I put my phone away. Lena will be here soon.

Maybe if I say it enough times it will come true.

Kasia smiles at me, and the worry fades away. Things can't go wrong on a day as good as this.

"He's nice," Kasia whispers to me as she puts a plate in front of me. I laugh. My father is no such thing. But it's good if she thinks so. She's had enough darkness in her life.

I won't allow it to ever happen again.

She will always feel loved.

She will always be mine.

Forever.

THE END

STORMY NIGHT PUBLICATIONS WOULD LIKE TO THANK YOU FOR YOUR INTEREST IN OUR BOOKS.

If you liked this book (or even if you didn't), we would really appreciate you leaving a review on the site where you purchased it. Reviews provide useful feedback for us and for our authors, and this feedback (both positive comments and constructive criticism) allows us to work even harder to make sure we provide the content our customers want to read.

If you would like to check out more books from Stormy Night Publications, if you want to learn more about our company, or if you would like to join our mailing list, please visit our website at:

www.stormynightpublications.com